You don't

DEAD

to work here... But it helps

Look out for the link at the back of this book for a brand new short-story absolutely free!

Contents

Chapter One 5
Chapter Two 13
Chapter Three.. 23
Chapter Four.. 32
Chapter Five... 41
Chapter Six... 47
Chapter Seven 55
Chapter Eight 61
Chapter Nine.. 69
Chapter Ten 74
Chapter Eleven 81
Chapter Twelve.. 87
Chapter Thirteen 94

Chapter One

Angharad woke irritably from an unsettled night's sleep. She thought she could remember having had nightmares, but nothing certain. Her name being called perhaps, and… no. That was it. That was as little as she could recall. It didn't sound like it should have caused her too much distress. There must have been more to it.

"Oh well, the day won't wait for me to make sense of why I feel so awful," she conceded to her cold, dark bedroom. Swinging her legs round and placing her feet onto the cold floor, she reached for the large woolly house coat she'd been knitting for the past three years and had finally finished. Good job, she shivered at the wintry October morning.

Cold had never troubled her much. She wouldn't have bought the icy, draughty house in the foothills of Pembrokeshire's Preseli Mountain range if it did.

It was beautiful, to a certain way of thinking.

'Like stepping back in time…' the estate agent's details had evoked. It certainly was. Dating from the eighteen hundred's it had received little modernisation since.

Open fires in each room provided heat, most of which escaped through the thin glass of the sliding-sash windows. Water requirements were met by a spring bubbling at the bottom of the garden for drinking and bathing, supplemented by a large water butt which collected rain from the roof for washing her clothes and dishes (and drunk by the numerous stray cats who had adopted her. They were a permanent fixture now and appeared to have come with the house.)

Filling a large terracotta pot in the pantry, which was plenty cold enough to out-perform a modern refrigerator, meant her supply would last the best part of a week, so she could usually choose the driest weather for its collection.

Sometimes, though, the rain didn't stop for days on end in this part of South-West Wales. Getting wet was no problem, she'd soon dry again, and the precariousness of carrying heavy water containers of on the soaked, slippery mud was a danger Angharad gave little concern.

She had enjoyed the summer, pottering around the garden tending her vegetables, milking Janet the goat (named after the lady who'd sold it to her when she first moved in), and collecting a small number of eggs from the three hens that bustled round the yard. It was all she needed.

Her electricity was generated from some solar panels and a wind turbine. There wasn't need to generate much—she didn't own a television and was meticulous about switching off lights whenever she left a room, and of course hot water and heating were achieved by burning wood in a range.

Summers were great. She would be out in her garden tending shoots, or if nothing needed her immediate attention, taking a stroll in the magnificence of the scenery surrounding her little cottage, as late as ten thirty at night. After such activity, she would sleep well and awake with the dawn ready to do it all again.

But as the summer turned to autumn, and the nights drew in, Angharad had felt restless with the drop in activity. Since two years ago, she had felt the same each time the seasons changed. Her melancholy had become so serious her GP had suggested she might be depressed and had offered to refer her to specialists.

Depressed! What nonsense, Angharad had argued. She had the perfect life. No-one to rely on but herself, no bills to pay, what more could anyone ask?

But the doctor had asked her to fill in a form of tick-boxes and had insisted his diagnosis was correct, drawing particular attention to her negative answers to questions of whether her life was worth living.

After storming out, the shock of what he had suggested had staved off the worst of her numbness for a while until spring had sprung from the chill of winter once more, and along with the budding plants, Angharad's mood blossomed in the warmth.

As winter approached this year, she recognised the same feelings of despair... no, no, no, that was far too strong, she was very lucky; restlessness, she decided was more palatable; and so set about finding something to occupy her mind.

The work of chopping logs for the fires, from trees on her land, was ongoing, but she found she always managed to be well ahead of herself, and lack of daylight prohibited most work outside. So, she had scoured the local papers, and now an exciting project, which suited her perfectly, had grabbed her attention. Today a response to her application to volunteer as a helper for the children's charity, Barnardos, arrived in the morning's post.

All the necessary checks were completed. Glowing references had been obtained from Angharad's previous employers where she had thrived caring for the elderly in a run-down nursing home on the outskirts of Bristol, despite confusion when her old bosses were requested to provide a reference for Angharad, as that wasn't the name she'd used then.

After retiring and moving back to Wales she had decided to return to using her given name of Angharad, rather than the anglicised shortening she'd gone by for years of 'Ann'. Angharad she deemed was more appropriate to her age and connected her to her Welsh roots.

The door to the bedroom groaned to her gentle shove and fell back on its hinges. Tiptoeing the short distance across the landing from her bedroom, she plodded down the creaky stairs to the kitchen, clutching the housecoat closed about her.

Lighting the main fire in the Simenei Fawr (big chimney), she hung a kettle full of water over it to boil. A cupful would go towards a steaming herbal tea, and the remainder would provide hot water for her ablutions.

Drumming her index finger on thin furred lips, she pondered another of the things she liked little about the colder months, other than the threat of insipidness; he dwindling self-sufficiency. Janet gave less milk, the hens, fewer eggs, and fruit and vegetables from the garden became very limited despite careful growing.

She knew today she'd need to venture out in the cold to the local shop which stood several miles away in the next village. Usually she would walk the distance, but today, as she had quite a lot of things she needed to buy, she decided to take her car.

Slurping the last of her tea dregs, she cooked the last egg with some slightly stale breaded soldiers, resolving to toast them halfway through breakfast in light of their staleness, by which time her egg had become cold. Shrugging, she ate it anyway. There was only so much time she could spare to devote to the most important meal of the day.

By the time she chopped logs, filled the water container, hunted for and collected eggs, and milked Janet, it transpired to be late in the afternoon. If she were to make it to the shop before dusk she would have to hurry.

Dead skin around her fingernails had a good chewing as a mild surge of panic filled her mind. Plagued by night blindness, driving in the dark was something she avoided.

Tugging on a woolly hat (another home-knitted creation) she covered her shorn grey hair, worn short-cropped for years for its practicality. Making her way across her potholed driveway, she slipped in the forming ice and struggled to regain her footing.

Stepping more carefully, she found her balance and rounded the corner to her car shed, a hap-hazard structure fashioned from corrugated tin nailed to old railway sleepers.

The car itself, a Skoda (from the era before they were much improved by VW), boasted being adapted to run on bio-oil—considerably cheaper than diesel at the pump. A magnetic sign advertised this fact in case other drivers hearing the sound of her tractor-like engine, and smelling the unmistakable odour of rancid chip fat, were tempted to convert their own cars.

After a lot of key turning and silent cursing, the Skoda coughed into life and Angharad was off. A few minutes later she pulled the noisy, smelly little jalopy into one of the parking bays outside the garage-cum-supermarket that served the surrounding area. She inserted her pound coin into the trolley release and went clattering into the shop.

"Bother!" she exclaimed, realising she'd forgotten her list. Aimlessly walking up and down the aisles, she plonked what she supposed she needed into her trolley. Scrutinising the price of prawns; deciding whether the 'value pack' was actually better value than the standard pack, she heard someone call her name. Not the name she went by now, but the name she hadn't used since her move back to Wales.

"Ann. Ann! Is that you?" she heard clearly. A shrill, woman's voice she didn't recognise. Shaking off her shopping mind-set to engage with whomever had called out to her, she thought it must be someone from across the border who knew her before.

When she turned there didn't appear to be anyone speaking to her at all and her cheeks burned in the cold. Other shoppers moved up and down the aisles, but none even glanced in her direction.

The confusion distracted her from her prawns dilemma, and she walked away without having chosen. Red faced, she stumbled self-consciously away from the freezer, hoping no-one had observed her muddle.

When the voice echoed in her head again, she tried not to embarrass herself by looking, but curiosity proved too much and she couldn't resist a peek behind. It didn't help. Still no-one looked her way.

Realising she must be hearing someone else's conversation, she took a deep calming breath. Humiliation turned to annoyance at someone being persistent verging on obsessive with their insistence at calling out to Ann.

Obviously Ann wasn't answering so Angharad wondered why they didn't simply give up.

The notion this could be a sign of early dementia reddened her face again, but only briefly. Partly due to her strong belief in her own capabilities. But mainly because the calling stopped.

She pushed the small trolley around, filling it with many more things than she remembered being on her shopping list. Cursing under her breath at her absentmindedness, she arrived at the till, still muttering.

"Hello Angharad. How are we today?" the pleasant woman serving inquired.

Angharad ceased her mindless muttering and turned to the cashier. With darting eyes, she struggled to look directly at her and babbled her reply "Okay. If it wasn't for that infernal woman calling out for Ann all around the shop! I kept thinking she was speaking to me."

The shop lady frowned at the reference. "That reminds me of last night," she said, her smile returning. "Oh it was brilliant it was! *'Medium at Large'* she goes by. Big, fat psychic lady. I've always fancied myself as a bit psychic, but last night was summin else."

Angharad wholly ignored her, placing the items from her trolley onto the conveyer in introverted disregard. Her thoughts caught up with her and she asked tersely, "How does someone calling out 'Ann' in your shop remind you of a fat medium?"

The shop lady took no notice of Angharad's unfriendly tone. She was used to her unusual customer and her odd ways. The remarkable time she'd enjoyed the night before mellowed her placid nature further.

"It's just, there was a time during the show when the medium was calling out," she explained.

"I imagine there must have been. Given the nature of the act," Angharad spat her caustic scepticism.

"Yes, yes. Of course," the shop lady agreed good-naturedly, "but it sticks in my mind because she was so accurate all night, but this one time…" she paused for breath. "This one time, she called and called for this woman, but no-one from the audience could relate, and in the end she had to move on. You could see it bothered her though." The shop lady, thrilled with her tale, sighed and drifted away.

Angharad didn't bother saying that in her opinion it was all mumbo-jumbo nonsense, perpetrated on the perpetually gullible and foolish by unscrupulous charlatans. She didn't want to cause unnecessary offence, and had little desire to change the woman's mind anyway.

An alarming pang of fear relating to her own passing gave her sudden goose bumps. As the first flush of panic swamped her, she forced it down. She had a long time to worry and consider what would transpire when the inevitable happened. Nothing, she sincerely believed, but it still wasn't very nice to think about. Hence the appeal of this medium woman, she supposed.

Once she'd finished packing and paying, the shop lady remembered the thrust of her story. She called out just too late as Angharad had already reached the door which had swished open in response to her proximity.

"The medium last night was calling out the name Ann as well! That's a funny coincidence isn't it?" Her comment went unheard, but she didn't suppose it mattered.

Chapter Two

Angharad sat in her drive and tapped the steering wheel. How was she feeling? That was something she'd always struggled with. Something wasn't right; she knew that, but was she shaken by the odd experience at Glandy Stores; or was she just relieved to get home before darkness really took hold?

Sighing, still unsure, she pushed open the car door and swung her legs out into the icy dusk. Taking extra care, she made it to the front door without falling and closed her eyes in gratitude. As she stepped inside, the house seemed darker after the half-light outside. Stumbling in the gloom to the corner of the room to fiddle with the lamp switch before the economy bulb slowly projected illumination, made her wonder of traditional centre lights were the awful bright monstrosities she always considered them to be. No. Of course they were. It was returning home in the dark that needed to be avoided, not her cosy lighting.

A couscous salad was promptly whipped up, to which she added four-day old Moroccan Tagine which had languished on top of the stove for days—a potential health threat in most homes, even with the heat emanating from the range, the ambient air temperature was low enough to discourage the growth of any bugs.

Finishing eating like a task to sustain her body rather than to provide enjoyment, she tipped the plate's morsels into the sink. The various cats yowled at one another for a share of the spoils.

Her trusty range seemed to take an age to boil water for her nightly camomile tea in her keenness to put this day behind her and snuggle in bed. Once brewed, she clutched the warm cylinder to her to the stairs and flicked on the light switch. It was one area that had a conventional bulb and shade suspended from a rose in the centre of the landing ceiling. Its position allowed it to illuminate both the upstairs landing and the downstairs hallway which, despite the harsh light, suited Angharad very well.

When she reached the top, she scurried to her bedside lamp and switched it on before rushing back to the landing to turn off the light there.

Undressing quickly in the cold, she wrenched her nightie over her head maintaining body heat by still wearing her trousers until the flannelette drooped to her ankles. Kicking them off and hopping into bed, she soon warmed, sipping her hot tea, cosied under the many quilts and blankets swathing her double bed.

Lifting the reading glasses which hung permanently around her neck, she perched them on her nose and picked up the dog-eared novel she'd rescued from a local charity shop. Finding the page she'd folded down as a bookmark, she read only halfway down when her blood ran cold, the novel falling with a thud onto the bare floorboards.

"Ann. Is that you, Ann?" the voice came again from the darkness.

"Who is that? Who's there?" Angharad demanded. She asked in a stern tone in an unpersuasive attempt to sound fearless.

"Ann? Ann?" the voice persisted. Angharad's tea cup shook uncontrollably in her trembling hand, spilling its hot contents on her lap. The thick night dress and blankets protected her from a nasty burn, but not from the shock. She shrieked.

"Ann? She seems to be distressed. We'll leave her for now. Okay Ann? We're going to leave you for now."

Angharad's heart raced. Chest pulsing with her rapid breathing was the only movement in her body rigid with fear. Minutes passed before she could accept the calling had stopped. The impression of a presence she'd been unaware of became conspicuous by its absence.

Still her cup rattled against its saucer as unused adrenaline and the chill of her bedroom combined to shake her violently from head to toe.

Who was going to *leave her for now*? Her mind raced, probing for a rational explanation. A concerned neighbour must have popped in to check on her in this cold snap. Yes! Of course. She never locked her doors, believing she'd attract thieves and robbers into her life if she allowed herself to acknowledge the threat. Trusting she'd attract what she believed, she had no need for home security.

Of course, no self-respecting burglar would consider Angharad's home an opportunity anyway. If they tried her door on the off-chance and found themselves inside, they'd more likely *leave* a fiver on the worktop out of sympathy.

When she thought of helpful neighbours there really was only one candidate. Apart from the people next door who had moved in a few weeks after her, there were no other neighbours within a ten minute walk, and even those were sporadically distributed

Her next door neighbours were living in a caravan whilst they modernised their home, currently boasting the same 'old world charm' hers did.

She couldn't recall their names but it was quite possible she may have introduced herself to them as Ann. Yes, she'd decided to be Angharad now, but it was certainly conceivable she may have inadvertently reverted. Next time she saw them, she'd ask them if they wouldn't mind not calling round to her house and terrifying her when she was relaxing in bed!

Feeling better with a plausible account, she drifted off to sleep even without the benefit of ingesting her fragrant tea.

Waking naturally after exactly seven hours at five o'clock, she opened her eyes to the cold and dark.

Last night's terror sprang to the front of her thoughts. Listening intently, it was with great relief she breathed out and acknowledged normality. No sound that wasn't meant to be heard could be heard. No calling of her old name. Nothing.

Settling down for extra sleep was something she rarely did, but considered it this morning after last night's disturbance had left her exhausted. As the light of the sunrise grew brighter, so did Angharad's mood. And so putting the terror firmly behind her, she fairly leapt from her bed.

Washing quickly, flinching from the icy wetness of her flannel, it was whilst drying herself with a scratchy towel she'd owned as long as she could remember, that her deliberations drifted to her upcoming plans.

Next week she could look forward to meeting the family with the autistic son. Her job was to teach him how to use public transport, plan a meal, shop for the ingredients, prepare it, and develop general independence skills. Her kindly face creased in a wide smile at the prospect. She loved to be useful.

There promised to be other families, too, with different needs whom Angharad would help over the coming weeks and months, providing her the satisfaction missing since her retirement.

Shuddering, she frowned realising it was last night's fright bothering her still. Dosing herself liberally with talc, she decided a bracing walk over the mountain today, while she wasn't too busy, would recharge her batteries and get her good and tired for the night. She always found it to be the best remedy for a low or anxious mood.

Opening her solid wood wardrobe, she selected appropriate attire; an easy choice as most of her clothes shared the same fabric and orange and brown colours.

The only decision was whether she should wear a jumper. October qualified as jumper weather, particularly on the mountainside she conceded, as she pulled on quite a thick one and packed a fold-up rain coat in a small ruck-sack along with enough drink and some cheese salad sandwiches to last her the day.

Approaching her next door neighbour's home with a stiff stride, she kept an eye out to have a word, but there was no sign of them. Scowling, she decided if she didn't spot them on her return, she might write a note. She would have to strike the right balance—firm but fair. She knew they meant well, but they had no need to worry about her. She was more than capable.

Lips curling in her assurance she was right, she pondered her decision to walk downhill when her plan was to go to the top of the mountain. Her eyes twinkled knowing how odd it must seem to anyone else. But she was in no hurry, and there were benefits a stroll to the bottom of the valley offered over a more direct route, and her heart raced at the memory.

Minutes into her hike, she thrilled at the swish of cascading water from the Eastern Cleddau River as it streamed down the southern slopes of Mynydd Preseli (Preselly Mountain). She crossed its bubbling white water over a small, iron footbridge next to an old, stone water mill.

The mill's function now, was to house Llangolman Slate Workshop. The current owner crafted amazing sculptures and useful objects, such as signs and barometers, out of the slate from the quarry.

She loved walking through the old works, which had been abandoned for more than a century, fascinated to witness nature clawing back its foothold over man's disturbance of the mountainside. It would prove a slow process compared to the speed of chiselling the rocks from their natural origins. Slow, but effective.

Another hundred years might well eliminate any sign man had ever been there, Angharad nodded to herself. Recognising the need to exploit the mountain's resources, she was gratified nature would ultimately win the war.

Following the river through thick woodland and down the valley, the sound of the rushing water filled her senses in a most delectable way that made her almost giddy with euphoria.

She had made this walk on plenty of previous occasions, but it appeared different every time. The autumn scenery might be her favourite, she smiled. Extra rainfall always meant the river flowed faster and the sight and sounds of it became even more stimulating.

Her heart leapt in expectancy of what she knew was to come, and when she wound through the forest and came face to face with it, she couldn't help but let out a laugh.

White water coursed down a cliff forming part of the quarry, perhaps cut into the rock to provide a tramway to transport slate to port a long time ago. It looked entirely natural now, and incredibly beautiful with the snowy spout cascading dramatically down its flank.

She knew a secret about this waterfall and set about taking advantage of it. Hidden by the white curtain, a cave could be revealed carved into the rock. Not by the natural action of the rushing water, but deliberately cut by the hand of man as a wonderful hidden room. It was tricky to get to, and she wouldn't have known about it at all but for her incessant reading of every single local guidebook.

Walking beside the waterfall, splashing her boots through the shallow depths at the edge of the pool, she ducked inside. It was as wonderful as she remembered. A delicious secret in an already hidden world.

She'd be content to spend all day sitting in the cave, watching the world go by through the curtain of crystal water. She could probably quite happily live there.

Imagining people walking past unaware of her presence, she giggled privately. Imagination would have to suffice, as she'd need to wait a long time for someone to come.

Sitting in wonderment, she debated eating her sandwiches now, delighted at the notion of a secret picnic. It wasn't sensible, she wasn't even hungry, so she sufficed eating a quarter of a sandwich and supping a few swigs of her spring water before leaving for the mountain slopes.

It grew steep quickly and she was pleased to have eaten a little. It would take another hour, at least, to reach the peak. Feeling the burn already, she gave herself the goal of accomplishing the summit before eating the rest of her food.

Onwards and upwards she climbed, passing large outcrops of bluestone. Resisting the urge to stop and touch them, she knew many more of the grey/blue boulders were to come, and governed by limited daylight, she had to get on. She laboriously reached the obelisk stone depicting the pinnacle of the range and looked out at the far-reaching horizon.

On such a clear day the views were vast. She recognised some of the other mountains in the distance such as Pen y Fan, the highest point of the Brecon Beacon mountain range, and the tallest mountain in Southern Wales or England.

Cadair Idris, and some of the peaks of the Arenig range near Lake Bala, extended distinctively skywards. Then there were many mountains she didn't recognise, and loved all the same, serrating the horizon. She supposed one of them must be the majestic peak of Mount Snowdon.

Sat atop the cliff near the summit, she dangled her legs over the edge. The vertiginous buzz of the lofty perch added to her lunch enjoyment. As she gazed about her, soaking up all she could see, she noticed the crown of rocks spearing out of Carn Menyn, the mountain visible from her house— the very same rocks, blue dolerite or bluestones, that were to be found at the inner circle of the mighty Stonehenge over two hundred and fifty miles away to the east! Much debate remained as to how they arrived there and Angharad hadn't decided which theory she agreed with. She just knew it was a fact that pleased her, as so many facts did.

She packed up the leftover food, which probably wasn't worth keeping, but she was always meticulous about leaving the countryside just as she had found it, and set off towards the other side of the mountain, toes pressing painfully against her sturdy boots as she walked downhill to the crags she'd been admiring.

Examining the sky, she decided she had time to explore them more. She couldn't resist touching them and as she smoothed her palms over the great tors spearing the sky, taller than her house, she felt peace.

Clambering over their vastness and admiring the far-reaching vistas the different aspects offered, she feared she had become carried away with her mountaintop adventure when she noticed the light fading.

She wasn't too worried, sure she knew the route home well enough to make it with her eyes closed. With a big breath, she took one last moment to enjoy the silence afforded by the lofty height of the hills. Eyes screwed firmly shut, she listened intently, the stillness washing over her.

Nothing to hear but the distant twittering of a skylark high above her head. No noise of cars, or farms, or people, or dogs, or anything. Just the skylark, and silence. Opening her eyes once more, she marvelled at the remoteness of her surroundings. You could spend a week up here and not see another living soul.

And then from nowhere, more chilling because of her remote surroundings, she heard the unmistakable calling.

"Ann…? Is that you Ann?"

Chapter Three

"Come on, Claire. Come on! We'll be late!"

"Oh, do stop fussing, Chris! It'll be fine,"

"You're the one who says you need preparation time. I'm just trying to help."

"You'll help by keeping me calm," she admonished. Chris blew her a kiss by way of an apology. Things could sometimes get tense as they spent so much time on the road together when they were on tour. On the whole though, they got on famously.

Chris had been happy to give up his job as a bus driver to ferry his successful wife around the country from town to city.

They were embarking on another sell-out tour of the South and South-West, venturing into the Principality of Wales for the first time on a five night tour. The city of Newport was the first date, then on to the capital, Cardiff the next night, onwards to Swansea, and then up to Aberystwyth before cutting back through the mountains to perform a final Welsh date in Cardiff (added due to popular demand).

After a weekend resting, they'd do a stint of another week in Wiltshire and Dorset before returning to their home in Essex.

The tour had been named, 'Claire Voyant, Medium at Large'. Claire Voyant had been her stage name since her career began decades ago. The 'Medium at Large' tag had been added by the television company who followed her on one of her tours after she began making a name for herself, due she supposed to her bigger than average frame. Quite a lot bigger than average, she had to admit.

She carried it well, it suited her, and was universally received as alluring. The television sub-heading had struck her as more than a tad corny, particularly combined with her own regrettable stage name, which had seemed a crime not to take advantage of her given name when she had chosen it. But banal as it undoubtedly was, it served its purpose. There couldn't be many people, in certain circles, who hadn't heard of her and her reputation.

She continued to include 'Medium at Large' in her promotional material to take full advantage of her minor celebrity status since the fly-on-the-wall documentary had aired. It had been a big success. There was even talk of follow up shows, and perhaps another series in the future.

In the meantime, repeats on various satellite channels sufficed to keep her popularity ever-buoyant. There was nothing more compelling to the ticket buying public, it would seem, than a recognisable 'As seen on TV' slogan.

"I'll start my preparations in the car, shall I?" she asked, questioning how late they were likely to be.

"If you like. But if we can leave in the next..." he glanced at his new Rolex wristwatch "five minutes," he confirmed, "then we might not be late at all."

"Well. Let's get going," she said, sounding convincingly ready to leave. In actuality, once she'd 'popped' to the toilet, re-applied her make-up, 'szhushed' her hair and gone to the toilet just one more time 'because she didn't want to stop as soon as they left the house', half an hour passed.

Chris was well used to his wife and had allowed an extra forty five minutes, so they were really leaving fifteen minutes early. He kept that to himself.

Claire left all the logistics of the tour to her husband as geography wasn't her strong point. After hours on the road (including two stops at services) Claire expressed surprise when they arrived at a very long bridge spanning the vast body of water of the Severn estuary. She expressed further surprise when she saw the sign welcoming them to Wales and its Welsh language equivalent 'Croeso i Gymru'.

"Wos that?" she asked in her strong Essex accent. "Is it like a different language then?"

Chris looked disdainfully at his wife. "Yes. It's a different language. It's called Welsh," he informed her scathingly but in good humour. Anticipating her next question he added. "They speak English as well. Don't worry."

The expression of mild anxiety forming on Claire's face relaxed again into meditative serenity. Chris forgave her ignorance, and was sure the locals would too. She was immensely charismatic.

They arrived promptly in Newport. Claire, oblivious to the extra time for the journey Chris had allowed, bustled, panicking, into the lobby of the hotel they would stay in that night. Chris and the hotel's porter arrived with the bags to be taken to their room.

"Mr and Mrs Sharpe," he informed the concierge. He usually checked in with their actual name rather than his wife's stage name. It wasn't that he worried fans would track them down; he had no intention of being 'Mr Voyant'.

They were given the keys along with directions to their room which was a beautiful suite facing the wide river.

Newport's famous transporter bridge could be seen from the window of their room, but it attracted little attention from either of the occupants.

Chris enjoyed a well-earned nap whilst his wife sat in meditation 'omming' in the corner. They enjoyed a meal from room service at around half past four before making their way to the impressive and modern glass fronted Dolman Theatre a little way from the river, and close to the hotel.

"Ah, Claire. Lovely to meet you," a theatre official proclaimed as they arrived in the foyer. "Would you like to see the stage?"

"Oh, yes please," Claire answered, and followed the man through the back stage area onto the boards where she would perform her psychic act in an hour or so.

"It's lovely. Superb!" she declared, genuinely thrilled. "I will easily see everyone. It's going to be great."

While she relaxed in her dressing room, crowds gathered at the theatre doors. The seats filled, and the hubbub of excited anticipation filled the air. There was about half an hour to allow the venue to fill before Claire was due on stage. Some of the earliest entrants were becoming jittery.

The importance they'd put on the possibility of a message from a deceased loved one was tangible. In reality, given the time constraints, most wouldn't receive a message themselves. For them, the reassurance of witnessing Claire's accuracy would allow them to further believe in an afterlife where the objects of their grief could live on. It seemed to provide a great comfort.

Over the sound system came the dulcet tones of the announcer.

"Ladies and Gentlemen. Please may I have your attention?" the deep Welsh male voice began.

"Could you give the warmest of Welsh welcomes for her first date across the water… I give you…" and in a much louder voice, "Claire Voyant- Medium at Large!"

The Newport audience (who had actually come from far and wide and some of whom bought tickets for the Cardiff and Swansea dates as well) erupted into a cacophony of appreciation.

Claire moved gracefully onto the stage wearing a light purple and white satin robe that had the effect of disguising her large frame, but more importantly of making her look quite holy. Once the applause had subsided enough for her to be heard she spoke to her fans.

"Oh, hello!" she called giving a double take, acting almost surprised they were there. Her voice was amplified by the sound system and her face magnified by a screen behind her. The audience chuckled their appreciation at the humour.

Claire understood it was best to get straight to business. She'd been inundated with spirits wanting to give messages to loved ones as soon as she got here. There was no point delaying things with more introductions.

"I've got a lot of spirit here," she said to her rapt audience. She closed her eyes a moment before connecting with her first message.

"I've got a man here. Very smartly dressed. Oh! He's changed. He's wearing an army uniform now. Not recent, no. Old uniform, First World War, I think," she paused. "He's showing me that it's hot. He's too hot in his uniform."

The audience bubbled with possible candidates but one woman in particular seemed to be muttering to her companion. Claire continued.

"His name is odd! Yes. He had one name, but was known by another… Jack. That wasn't his name though was it?" she asked. The lady shook her head, tears in her eyes.

Claire closed her eyes, evidently in deep concentration.

"William! His name was William." With that the lady broke down and confirmed her father, who'd been a Sergeant Major in India during the Great War had recently passed away to terrifically painful lung cancer.

"He says he's fine now, Darling. He's fine, and he's not in pain anymore. Okay my love? He's in no pain now."

A playful frown grew on Claire's handsome face.

"He's showing me a police helmet! Was he in the police, too?"

The lady shook her head but spoke up. "My boyfriend's a police sergeant."

Claire nodded knowingly. "Your dad says you're thinking about tying the knot with your policeman. Is that right?" The lady nodded, tears now streaming down her face. "He gives his blessing, my love. Your dad is giving his blessing to… Mark?"

"That's my boyfriend!"

"And who's Jane?"

"That's me," she croaked through her emotion.

Claire nodded solemnly. "William's happy for you both. Go forward with your dad's blessing. Okay, my love? Thanks for coming. You can sit down again now."

Brushing herself off as though the connection with William had drained her, she shook herself to full alertness and moved on to her next connection.

"I have a little boy. Blonde hair, he has. Lovely blonde locks. And green eyes." She looked around the room. "He's about… so high," she indicated just above her waist. "About five or six years old I think. He's showing me a red car."

The room remained silent. "Oh!" she exclaimed "Oh no! Oh no," she fretted. "He was hit by a big red car. Oh poor little man!" She looked genuinely anguished.

A young-ish couple stood, broken, holding on to one another in mutual support. "It might be our son," they rasped together.

"Who's Jake?" Claire asked of the couple, who confirmed it was their departed son, and that he'd been run over and killed a year ago today.

"I've got your son, Jake, with me then sweethearts. He says he wasn't in any pain. No. He's telling me. He didn't feel any pain. It happened so suddenly, you see?" The couple nodded tentatively in agreement, seemingly comforted by the information.

"He says; 'I'm with my granddad. I'm okay'. He's with his granddad, darlings," Claire repeated. The couple crumpled into further tears, barely finding the strength to raise a hand in thanks before returning to their seats.

Claire paused to take a sip from the glass of water she had on a table on stage with her. "Thirsty work this!" she announced, lightening the mood, to the appreciative murmurs from her audience. She couldn't afford to get attached to other's grief.

Striding back to the centre of the stage, Claire looked to be making connection again. "I have a lady with me," she announced. "Ann?" Several people in the room pricked up; until that was, she continued with the description.

"She appears to be about… late sixties?" Claire scoured the room for takers. "She's wearing clothes that could quite possibly be homemade!" She felt sure *that* would mean something to somebody. But people merely looked at one another blankly. Like a class of children failing to understand trigonometry, they gazed self-consciously at their teacher and back to one another for confirmation that 'no' this wasn't for them.

"Her hair is grey and close cropped to her head." Claire continued. The murmuring was becoming quieter and quieter. "She's definitely linked to someone here. Ann?" Claire repeated impatiently.

Staring out at the crowd for some corroboration from her audience, interest in Ann was undeniably failing to materialise. She checked her connection. Sometimes, her wires got crossed, but this felt strong.

"Yes, it's positively Ann!" she affirmed. The room remained silent. "No takers for Ann, then?" Claire probed one more time before being forced to move on. She ignored her strong link with Ann and allowed the next spirit its connection. It didn't take long.

"Who's Donna?" hands shot up straight away. "She says she loves you and is happy now. Does that make sense…?"

After the performance and post-show praise, Claire retired in agitation to her hotel suite where room service provided plenty of alcoholic and carbohydrate comfort.

"What's eating you?" Chris asked in amused annoyance.

"I don't know. That woman, Ann. I know it was a powerful connection. I don't know why there were no takers," she answered dejectedly.

"You've had dead-ends before. Plenty of them!" Chris teased, a wry grin on his face. "Why be bothered about this one?"

Claire feigned irritation at his mini-dig at her abilities. She knew she was good, and even on a great night she was likely to experience some connections that went nowhere. She couldn't explain her torment at this one.

"I don't know. It just felt really clear I suppose."

Without pausing, Chris came up with the perfect explanation. "I bet it was a spirit who has someone with tickets to another night, that's all. They were just being a bit over-eager."

Claire beamed. "That's it! Of course. You're a genius." She got up and smothered Chris's head in loud, wet kisses. He grinned as he endured the gesture from his relieved wife. She jumped on the bed with the tray of treats and tucked into a particularly sticky, sweet looking pastry.

With her mouth still full she spoke, spraying little bits of pastry onto the bed sheets. "You're definitely right. I bet she'll crop up again another night." She refilled her emptying mouth and allowed herself a little chuckle as she flicked through the channels on the hotel television.

Chapter Four

After a relaxing morning enjoying the hospitality of the breakfast buffet and the hotel's spa, Claire and Chris packed their bags and made their way to the Welsh Capital for the next date of the tour.

"Now, this is the Capital city of Wales, Love. See, it is an actual other country." Claire gave an enthusiastic nod to Chris, impressed with the information she deemed reserved for elite members of society. Chris, in turn recognising his wife's misplaced minor awe at his knowledge, shook his head in rueful incredulity.

They booked into their hotel, then set about enjoying the city's sights. Claire gushed with delight at the castle and the old white colonial buildings of the civic centre. She thrilled when she thought she recognised parts of the city from television programmes.

Al-fresco coffees were enjoyed on the quayside (even though it was getting nippy) and Claire felt ready for her preparations for this evenings show more than ever.

"I'm looking forward to tonight, Chris," she informed her husband whilst tucking into her second latte with biscotti cookie.

"Good. I'm pleased to hear it," he replied.

They made their way back to the hotel for beautifying and meditative preparations (for Claire, anyway). After which, with plenty of time available (but with the usual exaggerations from Chris), they ventured from the hotel to this evening's venue.

"I thought you said it was a new theatre? It looks a hundred years old!" Claire queried as they arrived at the antique structure.

"I said it was *The* New theatre. It's actually more than a hundred years old. One hundred and eight, to be precise," he enlightened from the information in the programme featuring Claire's beaming face.

They were greeted by the usual type of representative and shown to Claire's dressing room.

"I can feel a lot of spirit here, Chris," she reported. "A *lot* of spirit. It's going to be a good night."

The crowds queued and filled the theatre as every other night. The Compere announced the eminent Claire Voyant to the stage and instructed a warm welcome from the audience. Claire made her usual, gracious entrance. Everyone was welcomed and thanked for coming. And then, she got straight on with business.

She was pleased when her first connection came through strong, but also a little apprehensive because it was with Ann again. The same description was shared with the audience as last night, to the same lack of response.

She stood before an impassable torrent of anxiety. Ann, ridiculously, seemed to be an exceedingly rare name. It perplexed her, especially floundering at the first hurdle.

The connection was even stronger than last night's, and so she invoked a sturdy determination to push on. Creasing her forehead in avid concentration, determined to improve the clarity of her channelling of this particular spirit. Perhaps she just wasn't getting the crucial information needed to light the spark of recognition with someone in her audience.

"She's showing me something..." she paused as she struggled to comprehend what she saw. "She's showing me... prawns! For some reason she seems to be showing me prawns," she said. "Is there some connection with the sea perhaps? A fishmonger or something? Maybe a chef?" the audience mumbled in their joint failure to recognise to whom Claire was referring.

"Ann. Is that you, Ann?" Claire attempted, upping her efforts for clarity. "Ann? Is that you?"

She persisted for as long as she could. The connection effectively blocked all others. Her mouth dried as she had no option but to just keep repeating herself in desperation. Beads of cold sweat popped up on her clammy face. The audience faded in her hazy vision and the floor melted beneath blunt steps. With a gulp of despair she was forced to abandon the stage to angry muttering from the audience.

Chris walked on and did his best to explain how his wife had been troubled by the same spirit the night before, and how distressed she'd been. Unconvinced, the crowd sat in simmering silence.

Off-stage, Claire was back in meditation. Deep breaths, and counting backwards from ten to zero regained her that place within herself she strived to maintain. It wasn't too long before a real calm developed and she relaxed again.

Many voices from the ether jostled for attention, and she had no trouble making connections. After a deep steadying breath, she returned assuredly to the stage to a slightly doubtful audience.

Any scepticism was quickly blown away by incredibly accurate and poignant readings, one after another after another. Devastating body blows from the heavyweight champion, forcing the audience to take notice. They grew convinced easily. The precise material flowing effortlessly from the great medium had them mesmerised.

Apart from the initial hiccup, the performance proved to be one of her best. She took comfort in that knowledge on her way back to their hotel afterwards. But the whole 'Ann' situation had shaken her badly.

"It will all make sense soon, I'm sure," Chris reassured her. "It's obviously a spirit who's super-keen to be heard. I bet you'll find who Ann is trying to contact, and they'll be so moved and grateful, it'll all have been worth it."

"Yes. Yes, I'm sure you're right, Chris," she agreed. "I found it really hard to connect with anyone else when she was there. I wish she could just wait until the recipient of her message is actually in the audience. It would be a big help!" she concluded a little crossly.

Confident Chris was right, she couldn't help but feel apprehensive that she might struggle with her performance if Ann's interference became any worse.

Whilst Chris wound down with some mindless television, Claire closed herself into the bathroom. A few minutes later she came out looking perturbed.

"Whatever's wrong, my love?" Chris asked, tearing his gaze from the T.V.

"I tried to contact Ann again." Chris winced, vaguely annoyed. She continued, "I was struggling. I'm really worried she'll interfere with more shows." Chris shook his head disparagingly. Claire persisted, oblivious to her husband's discouraging gesticulations.

"I want you to help me connect. If you link with me, I might be able to find out what she wants... without the pressure of an audience."

She quickly cleared the little room-service table, putting the tray on the dresser out of the way. Chris was instructed to sit opposite her. Placing her hands on the cold, flat surface, Claire indicated for him to copy her. With hands arranged in such a way that their little fingers and thumbs touched one another, she closed her eyes and Chris followed suit.

She could faintly perceive a connection. It was better with Chris's help, but not much.

"Ann?" she paused, listening for a response, "Is that you, Ann?" She thought she could discern her answer. Questioning who she was. "It's me, Ann. Claire. You've been trying to contact me." There was no comeback to her reply. She listened closer, pressing the table firmer as if that would clarify.

"Ann? Ann?" she called out again. "I think she's frightened. Ann? She seems to be distressed." She gave Chris a decisive nod. "We'll leave her for now. Okay, Ann?" she called a little louder, as though lack of volume was the reason for the poor link. "We're going to leave you for now."

She moved her hand away from Chris's, breaking whatever connection they had achieved. "Well, that was a waste of time," she declared. "We may have succeeded in frightening her away, which might be an advantage to tomorrow's performance, but not to my sanity! I really want to know what the bloody hell she wants!"

Claire struggled to rest after her unsuccessful Mediumship and managed only a fitful night's sleep before the next day's travelling. When, in the morning, she seemed sleepy and reluctant to move, Chris decided that paying for a late checkout, would be a better option than Claire arriving at tonight's venue tired and in a bad mood.

He quietly phoned down to reception to make the arrangements. The hotel were more than happy to accept a small payment to allow their esteemed, minor-celebrity guest a lie-in.

When she eventually roused, she panicked at the lateness, flapping the covers off and rushing for the bathroom.

Chris knocked gently on the door, suppressing a grin. "I've arranged to stay for longer. Wanna go down to the pool."

After some clattering and banging from beyond, the door creaked open, revealing Claire's flushed face. "Oh you could have told me, Chris. I was in a right tiz!"

He walked away and sat on the bed, waiting for his wife to uncoil.

Relaxing in the hotel's spa proved just the ticket. They even had time for a leisurely lunch before taking the journey to Swansea later on in the afternoon. A glance at his passenger revealed she was back to her serene self. Chris smiled a self-satisfied smile and drove away.

"I'm in two minds whether I want to hear from Ann again tonight," Claire broke the comfortable silence after a few minutes.

"Yes. I'm sure you must be. You don't want her to interfere, but you want to understand."

"I *want* to help her! She seems frightened, Chris."

He nodded his solemn understanding.

They travelled in silence for a while along the motorway. Claire mentioned she was enjoying the mountain scenery as they approached Wales's second city.

"You'll love tomorrow then," Chris informed her. "We're driving right through the mountains. I think the road is even called Mountain Road!"

Claire smiled in appreciation and anticipation. "How long now?" she asked.

"We're just turning off for Swansea." They drove through the typical valley's scenery of row upon row of terraced housing lining the mountainside before skirting the city and heading to the marina. The impressive new homes and even more impressive yachts made Claire relax further into her professional persona.

She sometimes hated touring, but other times it could be very enjoyable indeed. Seeing the country and staying in lovely hotels wasn't so bad.

After their usual settling in, they arrived at Swansea Grand Theatre from their hotel in plenty of time. A crowd had already gathered outside and Claire signed a few autographs. It made her feel fantastic. Just the boost her ego needed. She was led through to her dressing room where she sat in tranquil introspection before curtain-up, as was her usual practice.

She wasn't surprised to find the connection with Ann stronger than ever. It was so powerful it again blocked everyone else. Claire was aware of other spirits on the periphery, but their messages weren't at all clear.

A sudden thought struck her, cleaving her face into a massive grin. Instead of letting it put her off, she would explain her predicament to her audience. They could help her! The crowds of like-minded people may well be what was providing the clearest connection with Ann anyway. Together, they might find the solution.

The announcement from the compare to the audience for the eagerly anticipated psychic to come on stage created even more cheers and clapping than it had on previous nights. She walked on to rapturous applause.

"Thank you. Thank you!" she cried, waving greetings to her fans. "Tonight is going to be a little different" she announced. "You see. I need your help." She took a moment to explain her difficulties with Ann and her plan for them to assist.

The audience looked more than happy to be involved in the unique experience. Claire took a deep breath or two to focus. "Ann...? Is that you Ann?" She could see her clearly. Somewhere up high. In an in-between land. Not on earth and not in heaven. Claire nodded to herself and to the audience that things were making sense.

Now she understood what it had all been about.

Before continuing her train of thought she decided just to confirm what she was sure she knew already. "Does anybody here know Ann?" The usual description of the hand-made clothing and short grey hair was offered. After a few initial mumbles the audience settled down promptly.

"Don't worry," she said. "That's what I expected. I think I know what Ann wants. She wants our help." The audience jostled in thrilled excitement.

Claire tuned in again to confirm her suspicions. "Ann? I can feel a deep connection with her," she reported to the rapt crowd. "She's very afraid. I think..." she gasped as her hand flew to her open mouth. "She doesn't know she's dead, my lovelies!" The audience, led by their mentor, gasped too.

"You don't, do you Ann? You don't know you're dead, do you?" She addressed the audience again. "She's in limbo, you see? She's tried to ask me for help all week but I've been a silly billy!" she rolled her eyes theatrically. "I didn't understand, did I?" She took a deep breath before letting the audience know what it was they must do.

"We need to help her go into the light. Here's what I want you to do. I'll instruct Ann to go towards the light. Then you, in row one, join in," she directed, demonstrating by pointing, who she meant. "Then the next row, and the next row, and so on, until we're all chanting, 'Ann, go towards the light!' Okay?"

The audience showed they understood with nods and murmurs and waited in tense anticipation. Claire began as she had said.

"Ann. Go towards the light." She pointed at the first row, who joined the chant for the next repetition. "Ann," they said in unison, "go towards the light." Claire pointed to the second row who joined in. Row after row grew the mantra which became fuller and louder until the whole room recited at an incredible volume.

"ANN. GO TOWARDS THE LIGHT!"

Chapter Five

Angharad couldn't move. Petrified to the spot like the vast Bluestones she'd climbed over for most of the afternoon. She forced her brain into grinding action to look for the truth. What was happening to her? What were the signs?

Somewhere in her mind she knew the calling she heard hadn't come from someone close by. She'd pushed out the notion of anything supernatural when she'd blamed the couple next door, but she had known really, hadn't she?

Knowing hadn't prepared her for the shock of hearing with an alarming clarity, 'Ann' called out here, high on the mountain. She had accepted that the Ann in question was herself

She didn't recognise the voice calling her, but she was sure it was English. Different regional accents troubled her, not having viewed much television in her life, but English, she was sure was right.

Then she heard something that chilled her more than hearing her name from a disembodied voice on top of a mountain in the middle of nowhere. It wasn't just that it was louder or purer than it had previously been. It was what it said.

"She doesn't know she's dead!" the voice declared, seemingly expressing the horrific notion to someone else. Blood drained from Angharad's taut face as she swooned in disbelief. Shaking uncontrollably, her mind whirred. It couldn't be talking about her! It just couldn't. She wasn't dead! No! She was very much alive. She patted her arms with her hands just to make sure.

Worse was to come. Rooted to the rock, she couldn't believe what happened next. Angharad quickly concluded that, far more devastating than simply hearing a voice call out, and understanding that the owner of said voice thought she was dead, was receiving a directive from the voice. It knew she was there. It wasn't questioning 'was it Ann?' It was telling!

Her head swam in a shark infested sobriety logic couldn't wade into. She was terrified to obey and couldn't imagine for even a second why it was happening. She heard the voice instruct her, and although she didn't know what to do, she thought she knew what it intended.

"Ann. Go towards the light."

The scream which escaped her filled the mountaintop. And then, the sharks of improbability closed their circling in her ocean of confusion and bit hard. The voice she had heard for the last three days was now joined by others, all there with her on the mountain.

"Ann. Go towards the light," they chimed in unison, like an invisible congregation. The chorus of the crowd more than doubled and then trebled again, all chanting the same dreadful command. "Ann. GO TOWARDS THE LIGHT!"

A sudden rush of energy allowed her movement at last. She heaved herself from the small rock to which she had been cemented and ran, stumbling over the uneven terrain towards the rough direction of home.

She felt she would never outrun the voices, but she knew she had to try. Her impetuous pace covered ground in a blur down the gentle incline from the summit.

The dusk that had fallen on one side of the mountain vanished suddenly in brilliant, blinding sunshine as she rounded the bluestone and faced the setting sun.

"Ann. Go towards the light," the unmistakable command called again.

Angharad froze. Momentum had rushed her headlong towards dazzling light now. Sunlight, surely? But the grotesque cacophony of the dreadful demand from the unseen crowd terrified her.

"Ann. Go towards the light… Ann. Go towards the light" again and again. Still trembling, she stole herself and took a step towards home, which was also a step towards the setting sun.

"That's right, Ann. You go towards the light. That's right!" she heard the English woman's voice encouraging her. Spinning around to confront her tormentor, she didn't expect to see anyone, but just couldn't comprehend what was happening.

Was it a joke? How could she see her, this weird woman with her ugly shrill voice? The chanting of the crowd continued but she could hear the English woman above them all.

"That's right Ann. You're nearly there."

She could cope no more. A whimper of defeat was lost in the deadening still air of the mountainside. What could she possibly do?

She wouldn't believe the voices were right, or even that they were real. But she was scared that if she continued her movement towards the brightness she'd be lost forever; that it wasn't the setting sun she walked towards and the voices were *not* some weird auditory hallucination due to her hormones or something. She might disappear into it, never to return, like a Universal gulp of breath into the lungs of the heavens.

What was she thinking? She was sure she was alive. Of course she was. She would remember dying, wouldn't she? She shook her head, admonishing herself for even half entertaining the idea that she was, in fact, dead.

Willing it all to turn out to be perfectly rational. Perhaps she should go to the doctor. Soon. She couldn't persuade herself. Legs shaking, her body wouldn't allow what her mind was trying to cajole. She physically couldn't take one more step towards the setting sun.

Collapsing in a shivering heap on the cold, grassy moorland, Angharad gave in.

"Thank you everyone. I think we've helped Ann pass into the light. She can be happy now." The crowd gave rapturous applause to show their pleasure and appreciation at having been a part of something a bit different.

Claire, in reality, was far from convinced Ann had gone anywhere near the light. The contact with her remained strong, which wasn't significant in itself. Most of the spirits she talked to were exactly where they were supposed to be. It made sense that she would still have her connection once she had passed over. But she just didn't feel that anything had changed.

Ann, wherever she was, at least remained quiet, and so Claire was happy to continue with her usual show.

It went fabulously. The unusual start appeared to have enhanced rather than impeded the performance. Relief turned quickly to contentment.

There was plentiful after-show attention from the crowd which she lapped up. When she and Chris returned to their quayside hotel, she was exhausted but quietly pleased with herself. The anxiety she still felt regarding Ann was easy enough to ignore. Fuelled by the sea air, she fell into a deep, refreshing sleep.

The sun had well and truly set on the mountain. It was dark and very, very cold. The voices had been silent for a while and Angharad at last had the courage to open her eyes and re-engage with her surroundings.

Relief was a perverse result of shivering with coldness. Despite the distinct danger of hypothermia, at least it meant she was alive. She'd never imagined an afterlife—certain that when you died that was that. Clinging onto any romantic ideas to feel better about the inevitability of death wasn't something she needed.

The last three days had made her question her innate belief, but, if there was some sort of hereafter, she doubted shivering would be a part of it.

She knew she had to make it down from the mountain. As difficult as that might be with the enveloping blackness, the temperature would get colder and icier before dawn. She smiled wryly to herself, knowing how her back to basics lifestyle had doubtless made her hardier than the average hiker.

She rummaged in her rucksack for her emergency torch. Eventually she found it under sandwich debris, paper napkins, wrappers and other accumulated rubbish. After rubbing some encrusted dirt from the lens onto her jumper, she switched it on.

It flickered faintly. She wound the dynamo handle and it brightened considerably; enough to allow her to walk home dodging crevices and bogs if she stopped every few hundred metres to wind it again.

It helped that it was a route she could probably just about complete blindfolded anyway. After a couple of hours spent plodding onward and downward she neared the house.

Arriving at the stone bulk of her cottage she panted with relief and even allowed a little smile to play on her icy lips as she stumbled inside. She lit the fire in the Simenei Fawr and thawed in its warmth.

A brief interlude of hazy consciousness proceeded a deep sleep, achieved thanks to the cold exhaustion overwhelming her exhausted body. Sleep closed in before she even had a chance to worry about what on earth was happening to her.

Chapter Six

"Wake up sleepy. We have a longer journey today," Chris gently primed his exhausted looking wife. "I can tell this sea air definitely agrees with you!"

She shot him a playful look of pseudo contempt and began the task of waking. Sitting herself up on her elbows, she attempted to rub her face and eyes with her hands, but found it impossible to do so in that position. She gave up, and gave in to a mighty yawn.

"Where's a bloody cup of tea then, Chris?" she asked, only half-joking.

"We're going down to a cooked breakfast in a minute. You can have as much tea as you like then!" Chris retorted. Claire mumbled to herself whilst squeezing past him to the bathroom and affably slapped him on the behind causing him to squeal in surprise and laugh in good-nature.

"I'll just wait here until you make yourself look a bit more human, shall I?" She ignored him and carried on into the bathroom.

Chris flicked through the limited channels available on the television in the room. He stopped when he recognised a familiar face.

"You're on telly," he called out. Claire peeped, soapy-faced from the doorway with a questioning expression on her face. "Just a repeat of the 'Medium at Large' tour."

"I think I've lost a bit of weight since then," she said, careful not to make it a question, because she knew it wasn't true. Or rather, it was no longer true. She had lost quite a lot in reaction to the shock of seeing herself on the square screen. But she had more than piled it back on again when, after an initial struggle, she remembered hearing that 'television adds pounds to you!' That was excuse enough to lapse initially, then fall into the same glutenous habits with wanton abandon.

Despite being rather displeased with her tubbiness on screen, she had to concede she possessed a certain beauty. Seeing the captivated audience helped to buoy her spirits and excite her more for the day's journey and tonight's show in Aberystwyth.

After a hearty breakfast the couple checked out and ensconced themselves into the privacy of their car. As they turned away from Swansea and onto the mountain road for Aberystwyth, Claire's thoughts drifted back to Ann. She couldn't help but worry, not just for tonight's performance, but for Ann's very salvation.

"She doesn't know she's dead..." The memory came from a dream that for moments after she woke, Angharad couldn't quite believe hadn't been a nightmare of the entire week. Waking fully clothed in the lounge with the fire embers still glowing convinced her that last night's eerie experience on the mountain had actually happened.

What did it mean *she doesn't know she's dead*? She wasn't dead. Was the message even for her? She had presumed because she was the one hearing it. But she wasn't Ann anymore. The voices had insisted on calling her Ann and not Angharad.

Where were the voices coming from? The most likely explanation was that this was the first sign of dementia or some other mind debilitating illness people of her age could expect to succumb to.

She had nursed people who it was almost impossible to believe had once been functioning participants in society, so desperate their need for care. Unable to toilet themselves, they didn't even recognise members of their own family. Some didn't even seem to perceive themselves. This was probably how it all started.

A pang of sadness and regret filled her heart. She had lived a worthy life, working caring for others. Much of the world had been experienced, engaging with other cultures as a volunteer helping those less fortunate.

There were small regrets of not having any children, but if she had, they would have left home by now anyway, and she wouldn't have enjoyed the opportunity of helping all those other worthwhile people.

Living a commendable life was no protection from the deterioration of age though. Many of the elderly she had cared for told amazing tales of their determination and achievements, sometimes through two world wars!

Captains of industry, Captains of ships and Captains in the army and police force, SRN nurses and doctors as well as astonishing nonprofessional careers too.

There were many, many children, grandchildren and great, great grandchildren they could call family, but there was no-one who couldn't find themselves victim to dementia or Parkinson's disease or some other devastating condition.

Her gaze drifted into the middle-distance as she mused over good times and bad, and wondered how many of either she had left.

It was late. The fire had died sometime in the night, but the living room was still roasting hot by Angharad's standards. She threw off the blanket she had pulled over her and sat up.

A terrific headache throbbed all over her skull. It was likely caused by not having drunk enough after her stressful walk in bitter darkness. The heat she was unaccustomed to must have made things worse, she supposed.

Hurrying over to the terracotta water butt, she filled cup after cup with cold spring water until her thirst was surely quenched, but her headache remained unabated. She fumbled in the cupboard where she kept whatever rudimentary first aid stocks she might have. Just a few grubby looking plasters, and some tablets in a bottle with a worn label, were gleaned.

Unreadable as it was, Angharad was sure the smudged word didn't say *Paracetamol*. A vague recollection of some long forgotten anti-biotics came to mind. She thought she might have brought them with her from Bristol when she'd moved back to Wales. Whatever they were, they were of no use to her pounding head.

She tut-tutted to herself as she realised she would need to venture out to Glandy Cross stores again for the second time this week. A frequency unprecedented in her self-sufficient life.

She wouldn't admit, even to herself, that she was glad to be making the trip. Apprehension gnawed her psyche as she gnawed at her fingernails. Her jitteriness revealed her reluctance to be alone. Dusk would soon fall again and she was petrified that the voices would return with goodness knows what instructions for her tonight. Nightfall was a good way off yet, but her apprehension befuddled her and made her unsure of the time.

She wondered briefly why the voices only troubled her at what she considered was the same time each night. She couldn't fathom, but didn't want to risk being on her own if it happened again.

The bio-fuelled Skoda was coaxed into life and Angharad drove the winding route to the shop. After parking badly, she rushed inside, eager for company. She only wanted Paracetamol tablets, but felt compelled to kill time by mooching round the shop awhile.

As she ambled aimlessly up and down the aisles, shock stopped her abruptly in her tracks when she heard something she couldn't believe. An eerie chill froze her to the spot. She stood trembling, gasping in disbelief when the same voice which had tormented her for days echoed through the store.

There was something odd this time. It sounded different; unquestionably in the room with her and not in her head. Looking round, there were a couple of other shoppers, and the woman at the till, she recognised as being the usual one, was looking at her, smiling, gesticulating for her to come over.

Angharad was in no fit state to chit-chat. Before the social situation became too awkward, one of the other customers needed serving and she was free to her own terror once more. Overwhelmed with her emotions, she hid between a stack of tins and a rack of crisps, covered her face in trembling hands and wept. What did it mean? How could she make it stop?

Then she became aware of something that was too confusing to be a comfort or a torment. She could hear the voice, clearer than ever. But it wasn't calling 'Ann' or talking to her at all!

"I've got a gentleman with me," the voice was saying. "He's wearing a blazer, and he's showing me a dog. A little fluffy dog." Another voice she hadn't heard before spoke next. "That sounds like my dad." And then the first voice again. "Who's Derek? Is that your dad? I have! I've got you dad here with me, sweetheart. Isn't that fantastic, darling?"

Angharad tuned out in sheer disbelief. She shook herself to regain her senses and knew the sound must be coming from somewhere. She followed her ears to the source. When she found it, she was more confused than ever.

The woman at the till was watching television on a small screen under the counter. Moving around on the screen was a rather bulky woman on a stage in a theatre. She was obviously a psychic. Had she just been hearing a television all this time? Giddy with relief, she laughed.

Respite was short lived as the impossibility of last night's horrific auditory encounter on the mountain being accounted for by simply hearing a television sunk in.

Even an unseen fellow hiker listening to the same program the shop assistant was watching now couldn't provide the answer. Certain she'd been alone all day, someone's television wouldn't address her personally, nor react to her movements!

The voices had definitely spoken directly to her. They had responded to her stepping towards the sunset instantly.

They called her name, well her old name anyway. There could be no doubt about it.

"Hello Angharad," a voice broke through her deliberations. Jolting, she gasped for breath before she realised it was only the shop assistant and regained her composure enough to appear relatively normal.

"It's amazing you coming in tonight," she said. "I wasn't expecting to see you again this week. You usually only visit us when absolutely necessary, right?"

Angharad's mind struggled to reply. Eventually she half mumbled, "I... er... needed some Paracetamol."

The shop assistant carried on, paying little attention to Angharad's attempt at answering. She hadn't really wanted to know, she was just keen to show her something.

"Oh," she said, attempting an appropriate response before turning the little screen towards Angharad for her to see more clearly. "I wanted you to see this; *Medium at Large*."

Angharad looked on blankly. "She's the psychic I went to see this week. Remember? You said someone called out for Ann when you were here last?"

Now she had Angharad's full attention. "*She* was calling Ann. When I was there! I tried to tell you but you didn't hear me."

Angharad struggled to cope. She couldn't join the dots to make a picture that made any sort of sense to her addled brain.

"Well. This is the woman. She's brilliant. I'm a bit psychic too, remember?" she blushed at tooting her own trumpet. "People have said I have a bit of a gift, anyway, but this woman, Claire, she's incredible. So accurate!" she enthused. "Watch this programme. It shows testimonials from some of the people she connected with spirit for. They're all amazed."

Another customer came to the checkout. The small television (actually a tablet computer) was tilted completely towards Angharad to scrutinise while the other customer was served. She watched agog, straining to understand. This was too much.

Chapter Seven

"Oooh. Isn't it pretty!" exclaimed Claire as they wound round twisting mountain roads. They had not long ago negotiated a large lake, and now were immersed in the green desert of Wales in the heart of the Cambrian Mountains.

The peaks grew loftier as they travelled north, but it wasn't the impressive heights that most enthralled Claire.

"Wos that?" she decried pointing skywards. After a quick glance, Chris could satisfy her curiosity and inform her she was admiring the national bird of Wales, The Red Kite, which after nearing extinction until the mid-nineties, was having something of a renaissance in the region.

It flew with athletic grace, curling one wing under, enabling it to spiral in complete mastery of the sky. A child-like grin of awe lived permanently on Claire's face throughout the journey.

When they crested a hill and came across the ocean in its turquoise majesty, she couldn't contain her excitement. "This is putting me in just the right mood for a fabulous night tonight, Chris," she said, bouncing in her seat.

They pulled into the seaside town and caught a glimpse of the old university on the seafront.

"It's the perfect setting!" she declared, "It looks like Hogwart's!"

Chris's squint relaxed. He'd worried this week about his wife and her preoccupation with Ann. Fingers crossed tonight would be a return to her normal unflusterable, consistent brilliance.

When the other customer left, the shop assistant turned back to Angharad, wondering how she was getting on viewing Claire Voyant's amazing abilities.

"That's the voice! That's what I've been hearing!" Angharad exclaimed in astonishment.

The shop assistant didn't quite grasp what she was getting at. "That's the psychic I went to see. Do you remember, I told you? There was an Ann she was having trouble connecting with that night. No-one in the theatre knew her either."

She did a double-take looking at Angharad. She would've taken a step back if she'd not been seated behind the till. The description Claire had given on stage in Newport and its similarity to her strange customer standing before her was suddenly very apparent.

"You mean, when she was trying to connect with Ann... That was you?" she hissed.

"Yes. I think that's the only explanation. I called myself Ann when I worked in Bristol before moving here," she explained. "I want her to stop. It's becoming really rather disturbing." Angharad felt shaky but gratified something finally made some sense to her.

The shop assistant considered for a moment before speaking again. "If you heard nothing until she started her tour of Wales, then when she leaves Wales again, maybe you won't hear her anymore," she suggested helpfully.

"You may be right," agreed Angharad. "But I can't risk it. This woman seems to have decided that I'm…," she struggled for a palatable word before settling on, "…deceased," shuddering at the utterance.

"She's trying to make me 'go into the light'. I didn't used to believe at all in supernatural shenanigans but… Well, it appears I might have been mistaken. In which case, I could be in grave danger from this Claire Voyant's meddling," she said seriously. "Who knows how far she'll go with it, and how successful she may be in getting me to pass over to somewhere I patently shouldn't be!" The shop assistant nodded in solemn agreement.

"You need to go and see her then."

Angharad gulped, hands fiddling with a loose thread on her jumper, unable to voice a response.

"I can help you if you like… find where she is I mean. I can't come with you of course. I have to work."

"You mean go and see her now?" Angharad winced.

"Well you could. You don't have to, but she won't be in Wales for long, I don't suppose. Maybe it would stop when she goes back home. But if it didn't, you'd have much further to travel to see her."

Angharad contemplated for a moment before announcing, "I suppose I'll have to then, won't I? If I'm to get any peace. If I don't, I'll be in constant fear of being dragged to the other side before my time and against my will."

She took a deep calming breath. "How can I find her? Do you know what newspaper it might be in?"

"Aberystwyth, tonight. Show starts at seven."

"How on earth do you know that?" Angharad asked, flabbergasted.

The shop lady chuckled. "Google" she said. "I just typed in Claire Voyant, and her Welsh tour came up as the top answer." She tilted the screen towards Angharad again to show her the information. She looked a mixture of impressed and apprehensive.

"You won't be able to get tickets, I don't think. But you could probably speak to her after the show." Angharad looked thoughtful.

"She's not going to be anywhere closer to here, is she? I usually go to bed early. If I saw her after the show it would be goodness knows what time when I got back."

"Cardiff. Tomorrow," the assistant answered in a flash. "You could see her before the show then. You could be in bed plenty early that way. But Aberystwyth isn't further from here, it's much closer. If you left now your ETA would be..." she consulted Google once more "... just before seven! Fifty three miles. One hour twenty seven minutes. Cardiff is twice as far."

An impressed and overwhelmed Angharad weighed her options. A little chat with this Claire Voyant woman might be better done tomorrow, despite the longer journey. It would give her the chance to prepare. Spontaneity had never suited her.

On the other hand, what if it happened again tonight, and she had to admit, it seemed very likely. Already sure she wouldn't cope, she was terrified what Claire Voyant might achieve in her attempt to 'help' her.

"I'm going now. To Aberystwyth," she announced decisively. "I'll need to stay in a Bed and Breakfast or something." Without being asked, the shop assistant presented a list of accommodation including prices and availability. She jotted a few down with phone numbers, and passed them over to Angharad to take with her.

"Thank you," she said before adding, genuinely not hinting but merely thinking out loud, "I hope I get back in plenty of time before my animals need feeding."

"I could drive past your place on my way here in the morning if you like? If your car's not there I could feed them for you."

Angharad was touched by the girl's kindness and gladly filled her in on which animals required which food. She thanked her profusely again and headed towards the door.

"You're more than welcome. Good luck. And let me know what happens."

Angharad nodded and went on her way without any Paracetamol. Fortunately her headache was much better now. Relieved to have a plan, she'd relaxed some of the tension, and some of the headache, away too.

She hopped into her little car and headed north. Dusk had set in already. Consideration was duly given as to how she might feel if Claire's voice spoke to her whilst she drove. She believed she'd be okay. The journey was to deal with that particular problem after all. Being sure what she was up against provided more than just comfort. It gave her a battle plan.

She hated driving in the dark. There had been no official diagnosis of any visual defect but she was sure she had night-blindness. After she drove past the lights of Cardigan town and out further north, she found she became more and more bothered by the lack of illumination.

The sea to her left and the ever growing presence of mountains beside her to the right confused her treacherously. She would be drawn to the beauty of the view in better light, but in the falling dusk, the mountains loomed, pushing her to the ocean like giant two-penny slots.

She swerved into the path of other cars once or twice before deciding she had no option but to stop and calm herself down. Her drive had begun in a panic from Glandy Cross stores and she'd become increasingly worked up. A few moments to do some breathing exercises seemed likely beneficial.

She had to put out of her mind hurrying to catch Claire before she went on stage. If she didn't, the stress of rushing might mean she wouldn't make it there at all. Slow and steady would have to suffice.

Noticing her hands shaking on the steering wheel and putting it down at least in part, to low blood sugar, Angharad thought she may as well take advantage of her time uncoiling to have a bite to eat.

She pulled into a lay-by near a café, but on further examination it appeared unfortunately to be closed. Remembering there being a few Tupperware tubs containing healthy snacks, and a bottle of mineral water rolling around in the passenger foot well, she hoped they were still edible. Luckily, the muesli bars and parsnip crisps appeared fresh.

Slowly she ate and sipped before settling into a comfortable position for a brief pause of quiet contemplation.

That's when it happened...

Chapter Eight

After the usual procedure of checking in to their hotel and unwinding awhile, Claire and Chris made their way to the theatre housed within the old University building Claire had admired on their drive in.

She decided with Chris to depart in plenty of time to walk along the promenade and pier opposite the venue before the show. Strolling down the seafront arm in arm, the lights shone brightly in the harbour and glowed in her heart.

"It's quite romantic, I suppose," Chris laughed. She made no response, so he glanced her way and flinched. Something was wrong. "What is it, love?" he asked. She took a moment to answer.

"It's Ann. She's troubled. I'm getting a connection with her but it feels different. Oh! It's rather peculiar," she dramatically proclaimed. "It's like... She's moving closer to me. Actually coming to me."

Claire was a very experienced medium, so she put on a convincing front of self-assurance. It failed to convince the person who knew her better than anyone though. Chris could tell that she was scared, and that chilled him.

He juddered, "That felt like someone walking on my grave, you saying that." She smiled at him, but he could see the fear behind the smile. "What do you think it means then?"

"I don't have a clue. That's what's bothering me. Something is not quite right with our Ann."

"But we sent her to the light last night, didn't we?" He looked confused.

"I wasn't convinced. She went somewhere. I don't know if it was where she was supposed to. I think the problem is, Chris, she doesn't know she's dead! When she finds out, I think she's gonna come and haunt me."

"That's not scary though is it? I mean you talk to spirit all the time. Ghosts aren't scary."

"It's on my terms. I'm in control. Ann is not pleased with me." She considered her thoughts. "I don't think she could hurt me. I don't really believe she wants to, but I've had some pretty unpleasant experiences, haven't I?"

Chris nodded slowly, recalling some of the less rewarding spiritual encounters he'd witnessed over the years. It stood to reason if someone was evil when they were alive, they wouldn't be the pleasantest soul in death. Claire had remained unscathed, if not a little shaken, by some thoroughly malevolent spirits. Thankfully now, she'd learned methods to keep safe.

Ann hadn't seemed like one of those, Chris pondered. His wife was uneasy because she didn't understand, and because she was afraid. And she had seemed to relish trying to unravel what it was Ann wanted.

Perhaps that was the problem. She'd thought Ann had asked her for help into the light, but her not going after all Claire's hard work meant the mystery wasn't solved, didn't it? And suspecting Ann was less than pleased with her was deflating for Claire's ego. That was enough to explain her disquiet.

Maybe they should talk it through, but later. He couldn't risk upsetting her before her performance. "I'm sure it's nothing to worry about," he said in his best attempt at a calming voice.

She smiled, wanting to reassure him too, expecting he was probably right. If there was something to worry about it would be apparent soon enough. Tonight she had an audience to delight, and she wasn't planning to disappoint.

The walk up and back down the pier was concluded impassively, their concerns distracting them both too much to enjoy the benefits.

When they reached the University, Claire turned to her husband, plastered the biggest grin onto her face and took a deep breath.

"It's show time!" she declared cheerily.

"Knock 'em bandy!" Chris grinned back.

The famous psychic arrived on stage to her usual enthusiastic approval. "Hello, Hello!" she greeted her fans. Immediately perceiving a rush of psychic energy, visions coming strong and fast. One in particular was taking shape. That's what she shared with them.

"Ooh! I can see a road. Quite busy, but there's a vehicle standing out to me. Has anyone lost a bus driver or lorry driver?" A few hands went up and Claire made relevant enquiries. She continued describing what she was seeing to the audience.

"I'm sure now, it's a bus. Not a red double-decker from London. I would call this one a bendy bus. It's concertinaed in the middle." She wafted her hands back and forth, playing the concertina. Blank faces stared up at her, but the vision was too strong to ignore. Claire persisted, certain she'd hit the jackpot soon.

A look of recognition came over her face as it began to take shape. "It's not driving the bus they're doing. They're not a bus driver, or a lorry driver. No. This person lost their life to a bus!" The audience gasped as one. "She's been run over. Oh it's horrible. She's just lying there on the ground. Oh, poor love."

Whilst several of the audience members had associated with passing family who were bus or lorry drivers, no-one seemed to relate to a bus fatality. Some of them wondered (and then berated themselves for their disrespectful thoughts) if the deceased had worn clean underwear that day, as mothers across the land were prone to warn.

It was a warning to live life to the fullest; and to live as you would like to be remembered. They all hoped, with no hint of disrespect this time, that this person had done the things they'd wanted in their life; that they'd taken the chances which made them happy before the advice: *You never know. You might get hit by a bus,* proved deadly accurate.

Slowly, arms lowered, their owners forced to admit with regret that this spirit wasn't there to speak to them after all. They each looked around the auditorium for other interested parties, keen to find out where this story would find its home.

Not as keen as Claire. She was becoming more than a little anxious again. She had an exceptionally clear vision of someone losing their life. It was unpleasant to witness even as a psychic image.

Where were the takers? Someone shy at the back of the theatre perhaps? Her eyes squinted, peering through the dazzling stage lighting to see if she was missing anybody, but was soon convinced that she wasn't.

Examining her ethereal image once again, she hunted for what she fervently wished would prove pertinent information to one audience member. Clammy hands began their clawing at her faith. Pleading with the powers that be that someone, somewhere was perhaps biding their time for the right piece of evidence before declaring their connection to whomever spirit was with her now, she struggled to maintain her composure.

"It's a busy street. Someone is there helping." Squinting even more, she tried to find more empathy with the scene. "I can't see who has died very clearly. I think it's a lady, but the image isn't sharp. It's rather blurry." Her attention raced through the vision to find something, anything, to clarify.

Angharad fidgeted in her seat. Attaining a tranquil state of mind was difficult to begin with. Then, all of a sudden she became calm and still, overcome with a peculiar, ethereal smog. It seized her very sense of herself until she didn't feel like *her* at all. It was an experience of being lost yet assured she was in the right place.

There came a sense of rising above her body, above what she usually thought of as herself sitting in her little car. Looking down from high in the heavens, she felt a lightness and a comprehension of truth that would have taken her breath away if breathing was something she was even aware of.

As her mind adjusted to its new surroundings, a vision entered her sphere of awareness. She couldn't decipher it yet, but it was becoming clearer.

Familiar with the concept of experiencing visions in meditation—some of her former colleagues had been what she had described as 'flaky' —she'd always imagined they'd simply dropped off to sleep and later falsely recalled their dream as a 'psychic vision'.

Was she in the middle of a dream? Not floating high above her physical body at all. Of course. It made sense, didn't it? She'd fallen asleep at the roadside and was dreaming. From her floaty state, she laughed quietly to herself.

The vision in her dream was forming readily. She recognised it and was pleased with herself. It was a bus! Why on earth was she dreaming of a bus?

The dream bus came closer and closer. She wondered what it meant. What could it mean when you dreamt of a bus? Different dreams were supposed to mean things weren't they? And not usually what one might expect, either. Shaking her head, she decided it was silly. Why did people always try to make things deeper than they were? She thought the obvious connotations were probably the true ones. That's if they meant anything at all.

Memories of a dream about a math's lesson at school came to mind. All the desks apart from hers had faced the black board. It clearly meant she was struggling with maths, which she had been.

Other dreams returned to her memory too. She, like most people, had dreamed of being able to fly. And after watching the film Jaws, she had been troubled by shark nightmares. She had even had the classic dream of being at work with no clothes on. And she frequently woke from dreaming she was falling.

Somewhere she had read that if you switch a light on in a dream it won't work. Either a room is already lit when you walk into it, or you cannot escape from the darkness. She had scoffed at the idea, wondering how anyone could possibly test such a hypothesis. She would love sometime to remember a dream where she *had* successfully switched on a light, just to prove them wrong. Typically she woke with no recollection of any dreams at all.

Why she was dreaming now about a bus, she couldn't comprehend. She'd used buses quite a lot when she'd lived in Bristol, but now, back home in Wales, the bus service made that impractical. She had relied on her car for years.

As she pondered its meaning the dream took on a realism she had never before experienced. The smell of diesel assailed her nostrils, along with burning brake pads, melting with friction. The squealing of rubber on metal, and the hiss of hydraulics as the driver of the bus stomped hard on the brakes, entered her ears as real as could be.

The assault on her senses horrified her. An awareness for the first time of the bus baring down upon her was an unbelievable shock. The image repeated over and over in slow-motion in her mind. All five senses alerted further to the danger as the heat of the bus burned her skin.

The utter panic in the driver's eyes as they met hers through the glass of the bus's windscreen pierced her core with their vividness. Closer and ever closer they came, but the noise of the brakes could no longer be heard, instead replaced by an eerie silence; leaving Angharad focussing on what she could see.

As the behemoth monster of the sliding bus neared her fragile body, the drivers face became too close to focus on. The image of his features distorted and mixed with those of someone else.

The 'someone else' took her full attention now. She struggled at first to recognise who it was, and then in bewilderment she knew her completely. She saw her own anguished face reflected back at her in the shiny glass of the bus windshield. And then it was too late.

As soon as she felt the hulking metal killer against the furthest extremity of her being; as soon as her annihilation was absolutely inevitable, it stopped.

From wherever she had been, Angharad felt suddenly herself again. As though submerged in a pool and finally breaching the surface, she gulped hungrily like a new-born taking its first lungful of air. Her entire body shook as an immense rush reconnected her with her physical self once again.

Sitting in her car at the side of the coastal road to Aberystwyth, she opened her eyes to the darkness. So disturbed was she by the images, so real to her senses, it was almost inconceivable to her now that she actually was where she remembered.

Panic shot through her; adrenaline surging around her body. She quivered uncontrollably with incomprehensible fear. With no option to fight or fly, the energy escaped from her as an enormous sob; her eyes streaming with huge, salty tears.

Chapter Nine

Claire focussed intently on the psychic image. She wasn't as surprised as she might've been if the bus accident *had* been familiar to any of the audience members when she eventually identified the deceased from her supernatural likeness.

Ann looked almost unrecognisable, but despite her horrific appearance from her fatal injuries, her face was still distinguishable, as was her shorn head and tell-tale home-made clothes.

Claire knew now why she had failed to connect the audience to this psychic vision. Why hadn't Ann passed over to the other side as Claire had tried so desperately to help her with? What she wanted, and what to do about it, Claire didn't know. She explained as best she could to the audience.

"I'm sorry. I know what's happening now. A spirit has been trying to contact me all week. She needs my help, which I will gladly give. We now all know at least how she died. Unfortunately though, I don't think *she* does. She doesn't know she's dead!"

The audience gasped their astonishment.

"She seems to be having trouble coming to terms with dying. Don't worry though. I'll get to the bottom of it. I will help this spirit. She's called Ann, by the way."

The rest of the show went by without further interruptions. Connections for many of the audience members were strong and impressive. Apart from her growing concern with what on earth to do about Ann, Claire was very pleased with the performance.

Angharad's sobbing abated with time. She wasn't sure how much time and didn't much care. She adjusted the rear view mirror to look at her reflection. Haggard, exhausted, sallow features peered back. What was happening to her?

Her own reflection in the bus's windscreen crowded her mind with every thought. Like a wallpaper background to any other idea attempting to force its way in. She had to make sense of what she was seeing and hearing. She simply couldn't see any way to go on with her life without understanding.

Whatever colour her ragged face had clung onto in her moments of abject terror drained from her features, as she recalled with a clarity she was usually unaccustomed in her addled thoughts, a numbing fact: her friendly shop keeper was the *only* person she'd had interaction with since Claire Voyant had called her name for the first time. And how many times had *she* said she was 'a bit psychic'?

Unthinkably now to her logical mind, Angharad couldn't even be certain she wasn't dead. A hard pinch of her arm hurt, but she knew as confirmation of being alive it was poor. She had pinched herself in dreams before with the same result. Upon waking she had realised that the old 'pinch me, I think I'm dreaming' proved nothing at all.

Foul tasting, bile filled vomit reached her mouth. She struggled, but swallowed it down. Was she dead? She had always believed that when you died you just ceased to be. That you were no more and just stopped existing. She didn't hold with an afterlife, assuming people just used the idea of it to make death seem more palatable.

She held that the argument 'life just doesn't make sense without it' was preposterous. The concept of a deity creating life for people to learn whatever it was they thought they had to learn, far from explaining it, made even less sense.

Some people she discussed the matter with even credited they were famous figures from history in a past life. She supposed that helped them feel important. But to Angharad, the concept of life following life had no more purpose than it simply ending.

What did it matter if these lessons were learned or not? Ultimately, she believed, it didn't give a point to life in any way. She had received no answer to her counter suggestion of 'Okay, who made God then, and why?'

Now she was confronted with a clairvoyant announcing that she didn't know *she* was dead, and the only other person she'd spoken to being psychic too! Should she re-examine everything she'd ever trusted and accept she was living in some sort of afterlife right now?

She couldn't be certain the other people in Glandy Cross store had been unable to see her, could she? Wasn't it more likely they were just ignoring her, as usual? Thinking about it, she hadn't been treated any differently than any other visit to the store. Her natural inclination was to keep to herself.

Straining to remember speaking to anyone else last week, she thought she must have, surely? The letter about her

Barnardos volunteer work had arrived just a few days ago on Tuesday morning. They wouldn't write to her if she was dead. But that concession offered little comfort. It was Tuesday she'd first heard Claire Voyant, Medium at Large, calling her after a night of disturbed sleep, and there was nothing she could recall to verify having been in contact with another human being since.

She could get out of the car right now. She could flag down another driver and ascertain if they could see her, and then she'd know, wouldn't she?

But the threat of confirmation of her worst fear was more than she could endure. And even if she could be seen, would that prove she was alive anyway? People saw ghosts all the time, and until now, she had believed them to be fools.

Sobs came violently to her throat. Fists from inside thrusting their escape. "No, no, no, no!" she roared. "I want to be alive. I'm sorry if I've been complacent since retiring. I loved being self-sufficient. I was really looking forward to helping the disadvantaged children in my new job. Oh why? Why? Why?"

Shouting released the merest fraction of the helplessness she felt. For a stalwart non-believer in God, who was she asking anyway? A sigh deflated her wracked body. Blood accompanied the pain where her fingers had been chewed to the quick. It might have given her something tangible to cling to, but she barely noticed.

She didn't want to admit that even though she didn't; hadn't ever, believed in an afterlife... she whispered it at first, and then accepted in full voice, "I'm dead."

The realisation left her cold. Why had she not known? How could she have died and not know? Her brain must have protected her from the horror and pain the moment she'd been killed. That would explain why she couldn't remember. Until now.

She imagined whoever or whatever came for the dead must have come for her too. She hadn't gone with them because she hadn't known, had she? And *that* was why Claire Voyant contacted her. *She* knew. An expert in her field, trying to help her.

A remarkable calm enveloped her. She understood, at last. And she knew what she must do. It was simple. She would go, as planned, to see Claire. But instead of asking her not to pester her with her nonsense, she would ask her for help—to pass over to the other side.

Chapter Ten

The audience cheered as the show came to its end. Mediumship is an unusual act to perform an encore. It's not possible to perform another song, or tell a few more jokes. Claire's only prospect of performing longer was entirely up to Spirit.

Usually forced by time constraints, and sheer exhaustion, to stop her clairvoyance after a few hours, at around half-past nine to ten o'clock, she found a brief rest to get her breath back in the wings often enough to give her fans another fifteen minutes.

As she relaxed, her thoughts drifted. The tour of Wales had only one more night to run. She wanted to make the most of the time. A romantic stroll back to the hotel along the dramatic sweep of Cardigan Bay with her doting husband would be lovely, now she had calmed down. It had looked so beautiful on the walk there when she'd been too preoccupied to enjoy it.

Thoughts again turned to Ann. She had to find a way to help her. Time would have to be made when she was peaceful. Perhaps tomorrow, she would sit and channel and find out exactly what Ann needed.

She waited in the wings, listening to the cheers from her appreciative audience. When Chris appeared on stage and announced his wife would perform awhile longer, the audience cheered even louder. Claire returned to the stage.

"Oh, thank you my loves." She signalled for them to settle down with flapping hands and went into her quiet trance-like state from where connections came.

"I have a man with me. He's showing me a fishing rod..." Hands went up, and she succeeded in thrilling her audience for the extra time.

She wasn't sure how long she'd been at the café lay-by, but there was noticeably less traffic now than when she had stopped. Angharad wondered what peril she was putting herself and other drivers in by even being on the road.

She pondered how she was able to drive her car in her posthumous state. Was the car supernatural too? Or, because she hadn't passed over yet, could she interact with physical things?

Her hands felt clammy and the steering wheel became cold and hard in her grip. She *would* get there and be okay. Claire would have the answers.

She had been very lucky, or maybe it wasn't luck. Perhaps guidance from a higher power had been crucial. Whatever the reason, she considered it most fortunate that the psychic shopkeeper was the only person she'd been in contact with.

If she had discovered definitively that she'd passed away, it would have crushed her. Claire's help was vital if she was not to remain in limbo forever.

Angharad started her car and joined the spasmodic flow of traffic. What was the time? She glanced at her watch. Just coming up to ten. She wasn't sure how long it would take to get to Aberystwyth from here, not being a familiar route.

Venue details had been provided by her spiritual ally in Glandy Cross. She knew to head for the old University building. With a thankful look heavenwards she prayed (her first time) she would be in time to see Claire, and to get her crucial help.

Road signs indicated her proximity to Aberystwyth and gave no relief to the nervous driver of the smelly little Skoda. Thirty three miles. About half way there. It looked unlikely she would make it.

Perhaps Claire would stay behind for after show drinks or something. At least the roads were clear. There seemed little chance of being stuck in traffic. If she could maintain the speed limit, her arrival should be in just over half an hour.

She passed some pretty seaside towns and villages but was in no mood to appreciate the views of the lights in the harbour from the numerous boats, eateries and public houses.

The little car ate up the miles. Journeying on, emotion became strong again. As she wiped tears from her eyes the danger of the visual impairment on top of her usual night blindness seemed less pertinent than it should. She couldn't die twice, could she?

Claire didn't hang around for much of an after show chat with anyone. She snuck out quickly with Chris. Images of Ann prized their way into the forefront of her mind, but she forced them aside; she didn't have the energy to cope with her, but the sheer persistence of the thought marred her enjoyment of their romantic stroll to the hotel.

Chris gave occasional glances to his wife's distraught face, each time he was moved to squeeze her hand. Struggling for anything to say, he eventually blurted out something just to break the silence.

"Tomorrow's show is a matinee, don't forget," he regretted reminding her as soon as he saw its effect. Claire stiffened and slowed her already sauntering pace. Considering her next performance even sooner sent a wave of nausea through her, forcing her to stop.

Bracing herself against the painted wrought iron railings which lined the promenade, she stared out to the dark ocean, the rhythmic rolling waves affording a hypnotic comfort.

"You okay, hun?" Chris asked, stroking a hand down her back.

Claire nodded. "Yeah. I think so. I planned to have some quiet time and channel Ann before tomorrow's show. That'll have to wait."

"Why don't you do it tonight? I could help you again if you like?"

Shaking her head, she said, "No. I'm done in. I don't have the energy."

Chris didn't argue. It was painfully apparent she was right. Hoping desperately the 'Ann situation' would sort itself out before she suffered too much more, he took her hand again. Pulling her gently away from the railings, "Come on," he said. "Let's go and give that mini-bar a seeing to!"

She allowed herself a grin. "That might just help, you know. It might just help."

After the third vodka cocktail from the little fridge, Claire relaxed. "What am I going to do about our Ann, then Christopher?" she asked semi-rhetorically. He shrugged.

"I have no idea, and I don't think you will either until you can put aside the time to give her your full attention. When we get home, you can meditate, ruminate, and consult Spirit guides to your heart's content. It's important you try and stay calm until then." He leaned over and squeezed her knee. "I'm worried about you, love."

That was the last thing she wanted. Swigging back the dregs from her current bottle, she sat up straight. "You're right. I'm letting this bother me far too much. Here's to a brilliant finale to the Welsh leg of our tour." She raised her bottle, remembering as she brought it to her lips, it was empty. "Oops. I'll need another one of these, please, barkeep."

Chris smiled and hoped the probable hangover in the morning would be worth it.

Helping her get ready for bed, encouraging her to drink plenty of water, he tucked her next to him in the sumptuous double bed. He smiled to himself as she snored gently in his arms.

An early wake-up call had been arranged with reception. They would be away shortly after first light.

The quiet road, more than Angharad's attention to her driving, allowed her safe arrival in Aberystwyth a little after ten o'clock. She quickly found the distinctive University building on the seafront and parked nearby.

What should she do? She imagined Claire Voyant would be finishing her stage show about now. It made sense to wait close to the door and try to spot her when she came out.

She didn't anticipate that being a problem. Having seen her on the little screen, she was familiar with Claire's appearance and without wanting to be rude, she deemed her larger than average build would make her easy to recognise.

She debated waiting in the University lobby, but several reasons made it a less than attractive idea. The fear she would be lost in the crowd of people exiting the theatre and overlook Claire leaving for one thing. Being forced to wait uncomfortably whilst she chatted with appreciative fans, another.

Mainly though, it was her fear of how other, non-psychic people, might see her. Or worse, that they wouldn't see her, and she'd plummet to a hopeless hell before she even spoke to Claire. Hoping she wasn't kidding herself and putting off the inevitable, she decided to wait and spot Claire when she finished talking to her adoring public.

Quarter-past ten turned to half-past as the first of the audience made their way from the University. Angharad peered with an intense scrutiny from her car to the door of the building. She watched with unblinking steadiness, as more and more people disgorged from the exit. She presumed Claire would be conspicuously last, but couldn't risk missing her.

Hundreds of people, mainly women, and some plenty large enough to fit Angharad's recollection of Claire's appearance, just to make it more difficult to pick her out, walked from the building to cars and bus stops along the seafront.

It was like playing real life 'Where's Wally'. Then the crowds diminished until there were just an intermittent few opening the doors and walking down the steps to the street below. The time in-between the doors opening and closing became longer and longer until they didn't open anymore.

Angharad could barely contain herself. At any moment the person who'd been calling her all week; the person who she hoped fervently would make sense of everything and send her on her way would walk out and make it all better.

But then the time dragged and dragged, and so began a steady disquiet that she wouldn't get her peace tonight after all. What should she do? Clenching her fists into tight balls, she pushed the rising panic from her temples and yelped in irritation.

She had little choice but to wait and watch longer. It was likely that the star of the show might want to unwind in her dressing room. She might indulge in an after show party for all Angharad knew.

Filled once more with tentative hope, she sat and watched the exit with fresh determination. But as the hours passed into Saturday, she fell unintentionally into a sleep fuelled by immense fatigue, and anxiety burgeoning upon madness.

Chapter Eleven

When she awoke in the light of dawn, she knew she'd missed the purpose of her trip to Aberystwyth. Repressing a scream of anguish, she sat frowning in silent self-contempt. Her stupidity missing the vital opportunity, which at the moment was her only hope, left her dumbfounded.

With a grimace, she forced optimism into her awareness and decided to be kind to herself. Whilst she conceded the delay was her fault, she had to accept it as unavoidable in this deeply perturbing situation.

A plan rapidly formed in Angharad's troubled mind. The shop girl had said Claire Voyant's 'Medium at Large' tour of Wales would be in Cardiff today after Aberystwyth. If she got to Cardiff, she could wait outside the theatre all day until Claire arrived if necessary.

She would have to steal herself and muster the strength to make the journey. She had no choice. Brief concerns for her little farm of animals surfaced. She was comforted the shop girl had agreed to look after them. A lump formed in her throat and she clenched her fists in anguish at the realisation they would have to manage without her forever. The shop girl would know what to do, she hoped.

The route to Cardiff was unknown to Angharad. A rather old AA Road atlas was consulted before setting off. She knew she'd need to stop and check it often, but for now, the journey began as a straight-up trip into the mountains.

The beautiful scenery made her wretched as she mourned her simple mountain life back in Llangolman. Driving through the unspoiled landscape in an emotional void. A vacuum sealed nothingness she scarcely existed within, on a voyage to a tentative truth.

Steep sided gorges through high mountains looming overhead won her attention only peripherally, and with no enjoyment. But from deep within, an ember of hope smouldered. As she journeyed, her nerves wrecked from the stress of what she had endured hearing for days, the ember grew to tangible theories.

It was understandable that, drained of energy, she might dream or even hallucinate the whole bus accident thing. It wasn't unprecedented to wake from a realistic dream in confusion. The added stress of her fretfulness over Claire Voyant might have caused her to be even more confused than normal.

She didn't want to admit she was clutching at straws and certainly didn't feel confident enough to put it to the test. And not enough to put off going to Cardiff.

In a cloud of self-deception, she journeyed onwards. Cardiff wasn't that far. She would have her answers soon enough.

"What a beautiful morning!" Claire proclaimed as she stood outside the hotel taking in the crystal azure waters of the Atlantic Ocean and its backdrop of the Cambrian Mountains. She took a few health affirming deep breaths before taking to the car for their morning's passage traversing Mid-Wales.

"Perhaps we should come back for a holiday some time. When you can relax and enjoy it," suggested Chris.

Claire grinned broadly, slipping her arms through his and resting her hands on his waist. "That's a lovely idea. We definitely should."

The alcohol induced slumber seemed to have benefited her as she sat serenely in the passenger seat making adjustments to her makeup in the vanity mirror of the sun visor. Chris smiled with relief as he turned the car left onto the mountain road towards the Welsh Capital a hundred and twenty miles away.

Claire oohed and ahhed at the scenery, the reverse of the journey they'd taken the day before. Chris was about to give more guide book facts about the area when a glance across at his wife startled him. He gulped nervously.

The troubled expression of the night before had returned. She seemed shaken up, the shock of the helplessness returning when she thought she was free from it unsettling her. "Okay, love?" Chris asked with another tentative glance.

Claire shook her head. "No. It's Ann again. But it's not."

"That doesn't make sense," Chris pointed out.

Claire's expression remained unchanged. "It's not 'Ann' it's something else! Something that sounds like Ann."

She paused with her eyes so tight closed the lids fluttered. The blue veins in her eyelids visibly pulsed. She resolved to keep her own thoughts from interfering, to decipher from guidance the name that had evidently alluded her all week.

"Angharad!" she suddenly exclaimed with unexpected zeal, pronouncing the Welsh name perfectly. "It's Angharad. Not Ann! No wonder I haven't helped her into the light!"

So elated to understand what had been causing her such difficulty, a smile turned to a titter and then to a full blown belly laugh as the relief of *knowing* what to do flooded her weary mind. Chris laughed too. His clever wife, happy and back in control, just how he liked it.

"If we make it to Cardiff in plenty of time, I'll sit awhile and help our Angharad to rest in peace once and for all," she announced in triumph. Getting to Cardiff early was compromised by the narrow roads, and the fact they had unfortunately caught up with a very slow moving car.

Round bend after bend Chris tut-tutted his way slowly along, acknowledging with every tut the impossibility of overtaking.

"Come on. Come on," he encouraged the driver in front in irritation. "Gaze at the scenery a little faster if you could, please."

Claire exploded unexpectedly in an animated flapping of her hand in front of her face.

"What *is* that smell? Eeww! It smells like… rancid chip fat!"

Chris noticed the plumes of smoke from the car in front's exhaust pipe. "It must be that bloody car." He nodded, indicating the leisurely moving vehicle they'd been forced to follow for a mile or more already. "It must be one of those bio-oil cars," he declared. "Good on fuel, bad on the old hooter!" He tapped his nose.

A gap in the road opened up after a tight turn around a steep round hill. An animal transporter lorry was coming the other way. Chris judged, with his heart pumping hard, that there was enough room to go for it... just.

He stomped on the accelerator, forcing the automatic gear shift to kick-down into a lower gear, and the car to surge forward with the added revs and torque. Just as he steered almost past the smelly little Skoda, it swerved for no apparent reason. Chris and Claire's car scraped along the high verge, the hedge clip-clipping the wing mirror and door sill.

The steering twitched out of control as Claire's passenger door almost scraped the swerving Skoda. Claire glared at the old woman she saw through the dirty glass window of the grubby old car.

Perhaps the shock of the situation clouded Claire's vision, but she failed to recognise the lady driver, who in turn, seemed wholly oblivious to the occupants of the overtaking car, and totally unaware of the swerve she had made that caused the collision almost certain to take place at any second.

With the squeal of the animal truck's brakes filling the air, the driver of the smelly Skoda braked too. In the nick of time the car slowed, allowing just enough room for Chris to squeeze their car through the small gap.

With angry toots of horns and Chris and Claire's hearts an audible drum beat, they were steering straight again. Claire shuddered with the release of adrenaline flooding her neuro-system.

"F...! That was close!" she decried unnecessarily obviously. Chris could only grip the steering wheel in ashen faced silence, trying urgently to regain his composure.

When, after a few miles, he managed to relax back to normal, he looked at Claire, horrified to see the look of conflict back on her face. He didn't need to ask what was wrong. But Claire spoke up anyway in reply to the un-asked question.

"It's Ann... Sorry, Angharad" she said. "I can sense her stronger than ever"

"She probably knows you have her name right now. She must be planning to make contact again," Chris suggested.

"That does sound likely doesn't it? But it's weird, you know? It was like she was just here!"

Chapter Twelve

Angharad saw the car zooming up behind her. She wasn't about to be bullied to speed up by some impatient so-and-so. She didn't deem it safe to go any faster in her anxious state of mind. As she turned round a twmp (small round hill) she was horrified to see the car behind edging out to overtake.

Ridiculous! There isn't room! You'll hit that lorry and kill us all, she judged, failing to notice the irony. She swerved to prevent the car from passing but, undiscouraged, it decided to pass anyway.

Confirming the danger Angharad had seen, the other car scraped along the grassy verge. Angharad concentrated on steering her own car straight on the narrow mountain road.

When she became aware of the looming larger car speeding alongside her, she stomped on the brakes, turning hard into a skid to compensate. The truck swerved and braked too, horn blaring. The idiots in the other car zoomed past.

She could do without incidents like that if she was going to make it to Cardiff in one piece. If she wasn't already dead, she soon would be at this rate. She pulled over into a convenient lay-by at the side of the road and tried to compose herself.

With the incident over, the full shock of it filled her senses. It was scary, but it made her feel alive. Alive! The idiots in the other car must have seen her car or they wouldn't have over-taken.

She daren't allow herself to hope. She was so muddled she couldn't think. Getting going again was all that mattered.

'Get yourself to Cardiff and find that bloody medium. You have to sort this out once and for all,' she drilled herself.

The mountains plateaued to a lush green range of hills that carried on infinitum, like waves of a grassy sea. The pair found it quite entrancing. Eventually, the hills parted to reveal a succession of large lakes—reservoirs formed in Victorian times by the construction of beautiful stone faced dams, providing water for Swansea.

The wilderness seemed to go on forever, but then slowly, the occasional home became visible, until the rural Welsh Outback gave way to gentle suburbia.

The character of the roads changed and became more and more urban, until the way to Cardiff grew clear. They would arrive in plenty of time for the matinee performance, provided the traffic didn't get too busy.

"I don't want to just sit in the car to connect with Angharad. I need to be somewhere peaceful and pretty."

"The mountains and lakes weren't peaceful and pretty enough?" Chris smiled.

"Yes, of course. But I didn't know we would have time then, did I?" she explained. "Besides. You *had* just nearly killed us!"

They drove near to the imposing colonial style civic buildings in the centre of the city. The formal gardens looked beautiful in the winter sunlight.

"Here will be perfect!" she announced. "Quick! Find somewhere to park!" she ordered excitedly.

A bus pulled away leaving a convenient but illegal space behind the bus-stop. Chris pulled in and jumped out to accompany Claire to the gardens in front of the white buildings.

"Head for that bench over there. I can feel her really powerfully, Chris. I'm certain that now is the right time!" she gushed.

Sitting on the stone bench, she was soon in deep meditation. After chanting for a few minutes, she requested out loud a connection with Angharad. She nodded and smiled knowingly, indicating she had a strong link.

"Angharad? Angharad. Listen to me. You have passed away. You are dead my love, and it's time to move into the light. Follow my voice and go into the light. Angharad, go into the light."

Whilst Claire sat, eyes closed, chanting on the stone bench, something else grabbed Chris's attention. It was that bloody smelly little car again. It had parked behind their car, slightly encroaching onto the bus stop.

He watched, bemused, as a grey haired lady exited, apparently in a fluster, clutching a mustard coloured home-knit about her whilst attempting to close the door with her elbow. He was alarmed when she gesticulated towards him.

She must want a row about that near accident on the mountains, he deduced, shaking his head in disbelief. She must be a right nut to follow us all the way here.

He strode towards her, keen she shouldn't disturb Claire whilst she was finally getting somewhere with the week's conundrum. He jumped in bewilderment as he heard his wife's shrill voice shriek from behind him, "Angharad! Angharad! Is that you?!"

After the over-taking incident, Angharad regained her composure and had driven along the mountain roads and through the lakes of the Elan Valley without seeing a single other car. She became confused as she made it onto the main road and had been forced to stop to consult her map.

Cardiff was sign-posted at most junctions so she wasn't confused for very long, numerous road-signs confirming her route. Before long she arrived at a junction that directed her into the city.

She didn't have a clue where the theatre would be that Claire Voyant was due to perform in. She thought she could do a lot worse than follow the signs to the city centre. The traffic was heavy, but it looked worse heading the other way. She mouthed a thank you to her newly appointed, anonymous deity. Her cheeks flushed at the hypocrisy.

Anxiety grew in her mind as she realised she was in the middle of a busy city without a plan. How was she going to find out where to go? She could just about make out the hand-writing the shop girl had provided as guidance if Angharad decided to go to Cardiff instead of Aberystwyth.

She had, of course gone to both now, but how could she find out the theatre's location? She might ask a passer-by, but part of her still felt uneasy she was not as alive as she had speculated after the near miss on the mountain pass.

She was still pondering, whilst negotiating the heavy traffic, when the all too familiar voice of her tormenter filled her head.

"Angharad, Angharad, You have passed away…" A huge sob of despair erupted from her taut lips as any hope the mournful messages for 'Ann' had not been meant for her, evaporated. The use of her actual name crushed that.

"No! No I have not!" she cried her objection. "Stop it! Stop saying that. It's not true!" she shrieked loudly.

Some of the other drivers stared at her screaming angrily to herself as they witnessed her through the car window. Pessimism made her sure they were looking because she somehow didn't look 'right'. That she didn't look alive. Tears of hopelessness streamed hard and heavy down her cheeks.

She was about ready to give up. But then she spotted something. As the imposing white colonial style buildings loomed, she couldn't believe what. The same car that had foolishly forced her to swerve uncontrollably along the mountain road was parked just metres away from her.

She wasn't usually one to shy away from telling someone exactly what she thought of their lunatic driving, but the same fear of how someone might react to seeing her made her incapable of action.

But then, she noticed something else. Something that must indeed be a miracle, what were the chances? Claire Voyant, looking every bit as large as life as she had on the small television at Glandy Stores, was sitting on a bench, apparently in meditation.

Once more filled with hope, she felt as a glass going from freezer to hob with her ever-changing fortunes—ready to crack.

She had to stop Claire talking to her like this. Why was she so certain that she was dead? Now she had her chance to finish this and make sense of it at last.

She pulled up behind the car that was parked inconsiderately in a bus-stop. But she wasn't there to argue about driving etiquette. As she flung open her door, the wind caught her off guard and swung the door into the traffic.

She scrabbled out best she could, holding her cardigan closed so she didn't blow away, whilst trying to close the door again. She just caught it flapping with her elbow. With a grunt, she summoned the strength to fling it closed, hoping the distraction hadn't made her miss her opportunity for peace.

A man, probably with Claire, or, it suddenly struck Angharad as more likely, the driver of the other car, strode purposefully towards her. A startling outburst of the same calling, unquestionably not just in her head, filled the vicinity.

"Angharad! Angharad! Is that you?" Claire Voyant screamed at her.

It all happened in a flash. Angharad perceived it in the slow-motion that these things always are.

The bus bore down on her as she closed the door of her car. It was, she recognised, *exactly* as she had seen before in her dream.

It got closer and closer, with her looking incredulously into the eyes of the panic stricken bus driver. As the squeals of the brakes and hissing hydraulics filled the air, and the smell of burning rubber and diesel filled her nose, Angharad noted in the slow-motion how faithfully it followed her dream.

Ah! And there she was. Reflected in the windshield of the bus as she had seen she would.

She didn't know, as no-one knows, what this moment would be like. The pain she expected was very brief she noted gratefully. She suffered the impact and felt herself fall, and then... well, that was all she remembered.

Chapter Thirteen

"Angharad. Angharad? Can you hear me?" it was a different voice, but saying the same thing. She was aware of bright lights, but couldn't discern their source. Then, the groggy realisation her eyes were closed. She braced herself to open them, unsure who or what she would see when she did.

Slowly, she squinted a crack, and then, when she recognised where she was, she opened them fully. A nurse was smiling down at her.

"How're you feeling?" Angharad didn't know. "You gave us all quite a scare. Do you remember what happened?"

Angharad remembered distinctly what had happened. She was about to get to the bottom of what Claire Voyant had been contacting her about for days when it had all become devastatingly self-explanatory. Well, almost.

"I was hit by a bus. I thought I was dead. But unless Angels dress as nurses just to cause confusion to the recently deceased, I suppose I must have survived."

Angharad's explanation was regarded to be a joke by the nurse who chuckled at the dry humour. She had been entirely serious. It was her way of thinking the situation through logically.

"There's some people here who will be very pleased you're okay," said the nurse. "They've been worried sick."

Claire and Chris timidly entered the cubicle whilst the nurse looked through some notes.

"I'll leave you to it for a moment," she said, turning to leave.

The pair stood beside the bed, unsure what to say. Claire broke the silence. "You're not dead. I thought you were dead, my love!"

Angharad looked at her, pleased to hear confirmation from someone, and a someone who ought to know, that she was alive.

"I know. I've been hearing you order me into the light for days. That's why I came to find you. I thought I really must have died, and I was in denial." Claire and Chris gasped in unison, staring at her in stunned disbelief.

"So you've been able to hear Claire—telepathically?" Chris almost stammered

"I suppose that's what it must have been... But there was more." She explained, "What convinced me most of all—that I must have died—was when I saw it," she said. "I saw what happened with the bus—precisely. I saw the whites of the driver's eyes. The last thing I dreamt, or whatever, was seeing my reflection in the bus windshield!" she stopped, breathless. "I had to find you. To make sense of it all. I thought you were going to help me pass over to the other side. When I did find you, I almost *was* killed." She considered her position a moment before adding, "How am I here? How did I survive?"

Claire explained, "It all happened in slow-motion. We stopped the car so I could contact you on the inner planes. I sat and meditated in the pretty garden. When I saw you standing in the road, I couldn't believe it.

"I thought you were a really clear psychic image, or... I didn't know what to think. And then the bus! Just like I had seen. I thought the whole thing was a ghostly image. An imprint on the past. It was Chris here who saved you."

Chris spoke next, "I didn't know who you were, other than that we had er… passed you on the mountain road… sorry about that. We were in a hurry…" Angharad didn't have the energy to react.

"I thought you had tracked us down for a row." He looked sheepishly down at the floor before regaining eye contact as the story took a heroic turn. "I saw the bus. I could tell, somehow, that *you* hadn't. I rushed down to you…"

"He was like Superman! The Flash. I couldn't believe anyone could move so fast!" Claire added proudly.

"I got to you scarcely in time and almost pulled you clear, but the mirror of the bus just glanced you. It knocked us both to the floor. When you were unconscious, I thought my eyes had deceived me and you had hit your head. The ambulance crew couldn't find any injury though, and you seemed fine, apart from being unconscious. We've been here hours. They even gave *me* the once over," he explained.

"Apparently you've had scans and things, which were all fine," chimed in Claire. "Shock, they said. That's why you wouldn't wake up." She looked Angharad up and down. "You seem fine now," she pronounced, matter-of-fact.

Yes, she thought. She was fine. At last she understood what had been happening to her all week, even if she didn't appreciate why. A broad smile which turned into a grin, then a chuckle, and before long, hysterical laughter, echoed in the room. She managed to say to the worried looking Claire and Chris, "Yes. Yes, I am fine now! Thank you very much."

The nurse re-entered the cubicle and spoke of scans, and doctors, and staying in overnight, but Angharad wasn't really listening. She was fine, and she was alive!

When dawn broke the next day, she was surprised she still had visitors.

"We couldn't leave without making sure you were alright, could we?" Claire said joyfully. It had been a difficult day. The matinee performance had been cancelled due to the unanticipated trip to hospital.

It wasn't just that Chris needed checking out, they both felt a responsibility to the lady who had come to Cardiff to almost meet her death because of some strange disturbance in Claire's psychic powers.

Since then, understandably, Claire had felt uneasy about performing again. She had nearly caused Angharad to lose her life. She needed to understand why before she could do her act again. This might not be just a one off.

Angharad smiled gratefully at them both.

"I haven't stopped thinking about you, my lovely," Claire began. "I don't understand what happened. Obviously I was having a premonition, but if you hadn't been able to hear me... Well, the premonition wouldn't have come true, would it?"

Angharad, surprisingly, had thought little about it. She was so thankful to be alive she had taken the time to rest. She agreed Claire was right. The only reason the bus vision came true was *because* she was seeking Claire out. But that was also the reason she was alive now. Because Chris had saved her.

A thought struck her. She formulated it into a coherent suggestion before seeking assurance of its credibility from her new psychic friend.

"Maybe I was *meant* to die. Or I had a choice. A predetermined time to die!" Claire looked intently at her. "I don't want to die. I love my simple life. I still think, even at my age, I mean since leaving work—I'm not old, I have a lot to give. "Maybe the way I was to die was... flexible," she suggested, incredulous at how her own beliefs had changed so dramatically since her first contact with Claire.

Claire was so impressed with the proposal her mind raced to complete it. "Yes! That makes sense, doesn't it!" she exclaimed. "Part of you wanted a choice, so your soul made you aware of the imminence of your planned passing... through me!" she was pleased with the explanation. It meant she had done good after all.

"The bus vision we both saw... It made you know that you wanted to be alive! It made you appreciate yourself and your life," she exclaimed, before adding, "It must have made Chris more ready to react to save you as well. Hearing how the bus had hit you. And Chris's speed. I'm sure a higher power must have been involved in that! You chose life. And we helped you do it," she declared triumphantly.

Angharad wasn't unreservedly sure, but she was happy enough for Claire Voyant to take credit for the whole thing. She had helped her more than she might realise. No longer was she scared of dying. It was something she hadn't realised she had been afraid of, but she knew now. If she was being honest with herself, it had been a constant worry since her retirement.

Now, she no longer feared the moment of death, and thanks to Claire utterly proving her paranormal abilities, she knew she would go on *after* death too. Maybe she would feature in one of Claire's future performances from the other side, she amused herself a little morbidly before taking an altogether more positive view, "But only when it's my time," she nodded assuredly.

THE END

We hope you have enjoyed this book

If you would be happy to leave a few words on Amazon or Goodreads by way of a review, or even just a star rating, that will be invaluable in helping other readers to find it, as well as helping the author to be more discoverable.

If you're happy to help, please follow the link.

http://viewbook.at/DEAD

Thank you.

Remember the link to a free short story mentioned at the beginning of the book?

Join the author's reader group for updates on new releases etc. and receive *No1 bestseller in Amazon horror short stories*, '***Frankenstein's Hamster***' absolutely free.

https://www.michaelchristophercarter.co.uk/no-1-hot-new-release-free

About the Author

Michael grew up in the leafy suburbs of Hertfordshire in the eighties. His earliest school memories from his first parent's evening were being told "You have to be a writer"; advice Michael didn't take for another thirty-five years, despite a burning desire.

Instead, he forged a career in direct sales, travelling the length and breadth of Southern England selling fitted kitchens, bedrooms, double-glazing and conservatories, before running his own water-filter business (with an army of over four hundred water filter salesmen and women) and then a conservatory sales and building company.

All that came to an end when Michael became a carer for a family member and moved to Wales, where he finally found the time and inspiration to write.

Michael now indulges his passion in the beautiful Pembrokeshire Coast National Park where he lives, walks and works with his wife, four children and dogs.

If you'd like to contact Michael for any reason, he would be delighted to hear from you and endeavours to answer all messages whenever possible.

mailto:info@michaelchristophercarter.co.uk
https://www.facebook.com/michaelchristophercarter/
https://twitter.com/MCCarterAuthor
https://www.michaelchristophercarter.co.uk/

More books from Michael

Frankenstein's hamster

Monsters can be small... And furry

Harvey Collins is a seventeen year-old prodigy gifted with a scientific mind that even has Oxford University excited.
When his sister's Christmas present of an adorable hamster falls foul of their alcoholic rodent-phobic father, Harvey is the best person to give him a new lease of life.
Using what's left of the hamster and parts of a rat and even himself, Harvey soon develops a pet like no other. Bestowed with remarkable intelligence and a thirst for revenge, Harvey's hamster is a monster in waiting.
Will anyone make it out alive?

Released just in time for Christmas, this short novella packs in Carter's renowned depth of characters and a thrill-a-minute read in a small package ideal for a car-journey to visit the relatives!

http://getbook.at/FrankensteinKindle

Or get a copy absolutely free by joining Michael's Reader Group (where you'll also get news of new releases)

Blood is Thicker Than Water

What is wrong with the water in Goreston's Holy Well?

When the vicar of a small Welsh community disappears after two little girls are murdered, Reverend Bertie Brimble steps into the breach.
His family are horrified at the danger he's putting his own daughter in. Especially as she looks startlingly like the other victims.
They do everything they can to keep her safe until Bertie himself begins behaving strangely, battling the worst possible desires.

And he's not the only one...

A terrible fate awaits anyone who drinks from Goreston's Holy well
Can Bertie uncover the truth about what's in the water before it's too late?

"Still reeling from the twists...

"Kept me thinking long after I'd finished reading..."

"The epitome of a great writer.."

Blood is Thicker Than Water is a remarkably thought-provoking horror tale from Wales's master of the supernatural. http://viewbook.at/BloodWater

The Beast of Benfro

Could the truth kill them all?
When struggling dad, David Webb, survives a vicious attack from an unknown creature in the woods, his fears swiftly turn to his flirty neighbour whom he believes might not have been so fortunate.
Calling the police only serves to place him firmly at the top of their list of suspects when she fails to turn up safe and well. Left to rot in jail, his only hope is his delinquent younger brother.

But as they get closer to uncovering the truth about the beast in the forest, they unleash a danger far darker: a menace which threatens everyone they hold dear.
Can anything save them from the Beast of Benfro?

http://viewbook.at/BeastBenfro

The Nightmare of Eliot Armstrong

Can you stop a nightmare coming true?

Eliot Armstrong, swarthy, handsome, head of history at Radcliff Comprehensive is jolted awake every morning; tortured by horrific, indecipherable images of a road accident.
Piecing the disturbing visions together day by day, he's horrified when he recognises one of the cars… his wife Imogen's.
Is it a precognition of his wife's fate?
Or is it a subconscious metaphor for the danger his marriage is in from his man-eating colleague, Uma Yazbeck?
He must do everything in his power to save his wife, and his marriage, But for Eliot, his nightmare is only just beginning…

Do you like thrillers with plenty of twists?
http://viewbook.at/nightmare

Destructive Interference
– *The Devastation of Matthew Morrissey*

Christmas will never be the same again...

When Matthew Morrissey takes an innocent stroll to his local convenience store to buy batteries for his daughter's Christmas present, he doesn't know it will ruin his life.
But, when he returns home, **everything has changed...** There are strangers in his home, his neighbours deny ever knowing him and he ends up attracting the attention of Bristol's finest.
Matthew has a theory about what is happening to him and who is to blame. But first, he has to escape.

Can he solve the mystery and save his family, or has he lost them forever?

Christmas will never be the same after reading this twisting thriller from
Wales's master of the supernatural
http://mybook.to/Destructive

An Extraordinary Haunting

The Christmas holidays can't come soon enough...

Swansea student, Neil Hedges is counting the days until he can leave his terrifying student digs and go home for Christmas.
For weeks he's suffered terrifying noises in the middle of the night and things moving which shouldn't. It's all becoming clear: someone or *something* wants him out! When at Christmas, a psychic friend of the family confirms his worst fears, Neil and his fellow students can't bear to go back.

But nothing is as it seems, and when beautiful former housemate, Elin Treharne, is plagued by nightmares of her one-time home; nightmares which reveal a disturbing and life-threatening truth, even she doesn't realise the peril she's in…
Only Neil can work it out and save her before it's too late.
But Neil can't cope…

If you're looking for a paranormal thriller beyond the norm,
you've found it.
http://getbook.at/Extraordinary

The HUM

*If you're paranoid,
does that mean they're not coming to get you?*

A strange humming noise, which seems to have no source, is tormenting the villagers of Nuthampstead, England, in 1989...
To the Ellis family, recently moved from the valleys of Wales, it has a sinister significance. They don't like to talk about it.
But Carys Ellis is only six, and she has to tell someone about the terrifying visitors to her room in the middle of the night when her family would not, and could not be roused.
And that's only the beginning of Carys's plight. Her mother is a long-term sufferer of a number of mental health problems. Diagnosed with bipolar disorder, manic depression, and borderline disorder, she's a drugged up mess.
And Carys seems to be heading the same way . . .
Twelve years later, beautiful loner, Carys, is pregnant. She's never had a boyfriend; never had a one-night stand; she's never had any intimate contact with anyone to explain her condition.
Not anyone human anyway.
Plagued by the dreadful humming all her life, Carys is convinced the noise precedes close encounters of the fourth kind; and that the baby inside her is not of this world.
She can't tell anyone. Her mum couldn't cope, and her dad's been relocated from Cambridge Constabulary to a

quiet Welsh village after a nervous breakdown leaving Carys struggling with her own demons.
Can she protect her baby from its extra-terrestrial creators, or will they whisk him away for some unknown purpose?
Will the demons who torment her get to him first?
Or, is she just a little crazy...?

Michael Christopher Carter's stunning portrayal of one family's struggle against mental illness and other-worldly threats is a masterpiece.
Described as "Life changing," this thoroughly well-researched novel is a must read for anyone curious about what exists both out in the cosmos and within our own minds.
http://viewbook.at/TheHUM

Printed in Great Britain
by Amazon